BRODY

ROCK HARD MOUNTAIN MEN

BOOK TWO

BY EVIE RILEY

CHAPTER ONE

Brody

IF YOU LOOK up the word "lumberjack" in the dictionary the entry says, "a person whose job is to cut down trees to be used in building and industry." This typically brings to mind the image of a man, often wearing red flannel, hacking away at the base of a tree with an axe.

Well, that image was correct in one way. I did often wear various colors of flannel to work. It was sturdy, comfortable, and easy to clean.

The rest of that image, however, was inaccurate. In the modern era, we were beyond the point of cutting down forests with hand axes.

First of all, a hand axe takes too long. We'd never be able to keep up with current demand if we had to cut everything down by hand one tree at a time. Instead, we used specialized equipment. Being a lumberjack wasn't just about raw strength anymore. We also had to double as mechanical engineers and operators.

Secondly, we couldn't just cut down any tree. Forests were delicate ecosystems that had to be protected, so there was a strict and complicated system for selecting exactly which areas we were allowed to harvest.

For this reason, I was surprised when I arrived at work and was told the location of our current job was being moved.

"What do you mean moved?" I asked

as I stood in the doorway of our worksite's temporary office. It was really just a shipping container that had been furnished to look like an office on the inside but was still clearly a metal box on the outside. The entire thing was easily portable, including the generator that gave the "office" power.

There was only one door and one window that had been roughly cut into the box. Standing in the doorway, blocking half the natural light, I cast a shadow over everything inside.

Including my boss.

Technically, his full name was Richard Fellsworth. He was relatively new, having been hired as our manager less than a month ago. On his first day meeting the crew, he'd requested that everyone call him Rick in an attempt to promote a friendly atmosphere. Unfortunately, he spoke as if he'd stepped right out of a corporate boardroom. From his too white teeth to his fake Rolex watch, nothing about the man was genuine.

I wasn't certain who started it, but less than twenty-four hours after being assigned as our manager, everyone on the crew unanimously started calling him Dick. He hated it and had tried numerous times to get everyone to stop, but the more he pushed back, the more the nickname stuck.

Dick was a physically large man who looked like he could have been a lumberjack in his youth. However, anyone could tell after two minutes of talking to him that he'd never done a day of physical labor in his life. His spine was too weak, both literally and metaphorically.

Despite the naturally cool temperature this high up the mountain, sweat still beaded on Dick's forehead. He dabbed at it with a handkerchief as he stuttered out an explanation, never looking me in the eye.

"Th-the order just came in a few hours ago. We're changing the location of the jobsite. Something about finding a protected species of plants in this area that we can't disturb."

I sighed, already knowing it would be useless to complain. Magnus would know more about the local plant life. If he were here, he'd probably have a million questions about what they'd found and want to see it for himself.

Not me. The only thing I knew about plants was how to cut them down.

"Fine. We've already got the machinery set up, so it'll take us some time to get everything moved."

"A... about that..."

I could already tell I wasn't going to like whatever Dick had to say, so I just glared at him in a silent command to keep talking.

"The higher-ups say they want everything moved in two hours."

"What?"

The whole office shook as I stormed over and slammed my fist down on Dick's desk. "Two hours? That's barely enough time to get everything packed up, let alone moved. What the hell are they thinking?"

Dick leaned back, but his desk chair didn't have wheels so he could only move so far away without looking like that's what he was doing.

"I don't know. That's just the order. They need everything moved within two hours."

"Well, where even is the new location?"

Dick pointed it out on a map, and I nearly blew my lid all over again.

"It'll take us forty-five minutes just to drive all the equipment that far. That's gives us barely more than an hour to get everything packed up."

Dick had his phone up to his ear, putting on an act of productivity even though he hadn't actually called anyone yet. "Look. I'll make a few calls and let them know that you need more time. Just get started, and I'm sure it'll be fine so long as it's clear that you're moving as quickly as possible."

I wanted to keep arguing, but there was no point. Dick was just a middleman manager. He may be the one to relay orders to the rest of the workers, but he wasn't the one who made the decisions. I had no choice but to turn my back on that cramped little office, slamming the door hard enough to nearly rip it from its hinges as a final punctuation on my anger.

"Two hours," I grumbled to myself as I weaved my way between machinery and stacks of already cut logs to find the rest of my crew. "It's a joke, is what it is."

I'd only just arrived for my shift, and I already wanted to be back home. The incident with the body we'd found and the

Mothers of the Mountain cult still hadn't been fully resolved. It'd been two weeks since Magnus and Trent returned from their last trip out to the hidden mausoleum, and so far, no one else had bothered us, but I didn't trust the situation to stay so calm. Although I usually enjoyed my job as a lumberjack, I would have skipped out on my shifts and stayed home if I could.

Unfortunately, we still needed money to live, and Magnus couldn't support us just by moonlighting as a cage fighter.

The other lumberjacks on duty were, unsurprisingly, just as upset by the order as I was. After shouting complaints for a few minutes—and other less savory threats—we eventually decide to just say "fuck it" and start getting everything moved.

The higher-ups were undoubtedly going to be upset when we couldn't meet their impossible deadline, but what could they actually do about it?

If they fired us, then they'd have to move the equipment themselves, and the prissy little suits that owned the logging company would never do that.

In the end, we managed to get everything moved over to the new site in less than four hours, which was already a miracle. When Dick came out to inspect the work after his office space was set up again, he had a phone held up to his ear. I could tell from the expression on his face that whoever was on the other line was probably yelling at him to speed things up.

"They want us to start on the north side," he said while covering the speaker of his phone with one hand.

I'd just looked at the surveyor's map, so I already had a good idea of the landscape, but I double-checked it again just to be sure. "That area's on a steep slope. Anything we cut there is going to roll. It would be better to start on the south side where the land is flatter."

Before I'd even finished, Dick was already shaking his head.

"The south side is too dense. We'd have to clear things out first in order to get the machines out there. There'd be no actual productivity until tomorrow. Start on the north side and harvest what lumber you can while we get another team to start clearing out the south side."

It was a terrible plan. There was no way we'd have enough time to properly survey the lower side of the slope. We'd basically be cutting down trees and letting them fall blindly, hoping they didn't land on anything.

Dick turned away from me, talking into his phone to assure whomever he was talking to that we would follow their orders.

I grabbed his shoulder and forcibly turned him around, so he'd have no choice but to hear me.

"I want it in writing."

"What?" He scowled, but then his eyes trailed up to look at me, reminding him of our height difference. Dick wasn't a small man. He probably wasn't used to having to raise his eyes to meet someone's gaze.

"I want these orders in writing. If you want to rush and do things out of order, fine. But I won't be held responsible if anything goes wrong, so I want this order in writing." I crossed my arms over my chest in a move that I knew emphasized the scars crisscrossing over my forearms and the general width of my shoulders.

Dick instinctively took a step back.

"All right. Fine. I'll get an email sent to you. Just... get started on your job."

His last words were probably meant to be a command, but they lost all authority as he scurried away and darted back into the safety of his office.

Laughing quietly to myself, I let my

shoulders slump.

I'd put on some weight in the last few years, especially after retiring from the military. The flat stomach and chiseled physique I'd once had during my boot camp days were a long-forgotten memory, replaced by love handles and a soft stomach. I didn't feel as powerful as I had in my youth, but apparently, I could still put up an intimidating appearance when I wanted.

Oh well.

What else could I expect at forty-six years old?

At least I was still more fit than most, and perfectly capable of doing my job.

It was well past noon when the first tree fell. Much later than usual, though sooner than I expected. Our work progressed slowly, as we were trying to set up and move forward at the same time.

I usually preferred to be on the front lines of manual labor, running the machines or hooking chains around the newly felled logs to haul them away. I especially preferred the moments when I could pick up an axe or saw and hack away at the wooden trunk with the strength of my own hands.

Today was not that kind of day.

We were on a time crunch, so I jumped behind the controls of a harvester machine and got to work cutting down whatever trees were within safe reach.

Since we'd moved to a new area, there wasn't much open space yet. That would change as we cleared out more of the trees, but for now, we were still surrounded on all sides by a towering wall of greenery. The shadow of the canopy cooled the area by at least an extra ten degrees, and never let the forest floor property dry out, so there was a constant smell of clean, damp earth and fresh pine.

The control cage of the harvester vibrated around me as the saws bit into the wood of the next tree, and with each passing moment, I felt the irritation draining out of me. I shouldn't have gotten so angry earlier. The whole reason I'd chosen to work for this company was because of their dedication to sustainable logging. A less ethical company would have simply ignored the presence of protected plant life and continued harvesting the area as planned. I should be thankful that my bosses were willing to uproot and move their whole operation to protect the forest around us.

If only they didn't try to make up for their losses by putting impossible demands on their workers.

There was a shift in the controls under my hands as the saws of the machine finished cutting through the tree trunk, and I pulled the harvester back. Ropes, which had already been tied to the trunk, directed it to fall in a safe direction away from the works, but there was always an element of unpredictability once gravity took over.

With a resounding crash, the large tree trunk hit the ground, crushing smaller bushes that there hadn't been time to clear away under its weight.

At that exact same moment, my phone started ringing. The ringtone was barely audible over the noise of the falling tree and other nearby machinery, but the moment those familiar musical notes reached my ears I instantly darted my hand down to the phone at my hip.

That ringtone was connected to only two numbers. Magnus and Creed. No matter what was going on, even when I was in the middle of work, I would always pick up their call.

"Creed," I greeted once I'd looked at which number was calling. "I'm working right now so I can't talk long. What'd you need?"

Creed's familiar voice was undercut

with static when he spoke, an unfortunate effect from the many miles that separated us.

"Any more news about the body?"

He didn't need to specify which one.

"No. We're certain that the body isn't Jacob Thornley like we originally thought, but they still haven't managed to identify who it belongs to. Although, I don't think authorities are trying very hard. A cold case more than a hundred years old isn't exactly a priority, especially when they aren't even certain if a crime actually happened."

The static picked up, completely cutting off his voice for a moment, but I still caught the end of his statement.

"...no one buries a body under concrete for no reason."

"Probably not," I agreed. "But so far, we've got things handled. It's fine."

Magnus and I had mutually agreed not to tell Creed about his last trip out to the secret mausoleum. If Creed knew that Magnus had been drugged and left wandering around the forest hallucinating for an unknown about of time, he'd probably do something drastic. Going AWOL to sneak back stateside and check on Magnus for himself was not outside the realm of possibility for Creed. The man was a walking bundle of extremes, always running either too hot or too cold. He didn't need that kind of distraction during his last few months of service.

In the background of the phone call, I could hear the faint sound of a pen scratching over paper. Creed tended to doodle when he was nervous. It was an oddly endearing habit for the otherwise intense man, and a clear sign that he was more stressed over the situation that he was willing to admit.

"Still, I hate that you guys are dealing with all this without me there. I've asked around about a way to get discharged early, but so far, no luck."

His voice twisted tight with frustration until he was merely grumbling under his breath. Creed wasn't a man who was regularly told no. He had a way of always getting what he wanted, one way or another, even if he had to strong-arm the solution into existence. However, military bureaucracy was a different kind of monster. No amount of threatening would make it bend to his will.

"What?" I laughed, trying to lighten the mood. "You think we can't handle one dead body without you? Or are you jealous that you're missing out on the fun? Military life's gotten too boring for you?"

Although I couldn't see Creed, I could easily picture his stony expression and the way he was probably crossing his arms right now.

"Shut up. I'd prefer a little boredom. They're sending me out on another mission soon."

"Oh?" I sat up straighter behind the controls of the harvester. "How long?"

"Don't know. Don't have all the details yet, but I'll probably be out of contact for a while. I don't want to say this'll be my last mission, but..."

Creed was retiring in just a few months. If this upcoming mission was as big as he was implying, it would likely eat up the last of his service time. However, calling something your "last mission" out loud was just asking for trouble.

"Be careful," I said, putting as much weight behind my words as I could. "Don't do anything stupid. Just keep your head down, do your job, and get out. This is a three-man operation that Magnus and I are trying to set up by ourselves. We need you here."

"Hey. You know me. When have I ever done anything stupid?"

"Do you want that list alphabetically or

chronologically?"

"Ah, fuck off. You and Mag take care of yourselves, and I'll talk to you later."

After saying our goodbyes, the phone line went dead, and I stared at the black screen with a heavy heart. Magnus, Creed, and I had met early in our military careers, and always had each other's backs from that point on. It certainly wasn't the first time we'd been on different missions, but it was our longest stint of separation.

I felt unbalanced. A third of my life was missing, and I couldn't do anything about it.

It was a miracle that Magnus and I managed to retire at the same time, but I couldn't help being greedy and wishing that Creed could have come with us as well.

I was pulled out of my thoughts by the sound of sudden shouting. One of the other machines up ahead had come to a sudden stop, and at least a dozen people were running around in all directions.

Sighing, I turned off my own machine and jumped down from the controls to see what the problem was. I grabbed one of the more experienced lumberjacks as he was running by and demanded to know what was happening. This man had spent most of his life working as a logger. He'd seen just about every emergency this job could dish out.

Yet, there was fear in his eyes now.

"What's wrong?" I demanded again when he didn't answer me the first time.

"We didn't..." He pointed out past the line of freshly cut trees. "We didn't know anyone was there."

I started running, dragging the other man along with me.

He tripped over his feet as he tried to stay with me while also continuing to explain. "They must have been camping out here illegally. The whole area is restricted. No one's allowed out here. We had no reason to double check."

Charging through mud and vaulting over fallen logs, I quickly arrived on the scene. Several people stood at the edge of a small cliff, about thirty feet high. We were working on a slope, and just as I'd predicted earlier, some of the fallen trees rolled downhill once cut. It shouldn't have been a problem since all our workers were carefully stationed uphill, but one of the logs had slid far enough to tumble right over the edge of the cliff.

Down below, I could just see the colorful canvas of a smashed tent sticking out under the body of the fallen trunk.

"Fuck! What are you all just standing around for?"

Grabbing onto the lip of the cliff, I swung my body over the edge.

Several hands tried to grab me at once.

"What are you doing?" someone shouted.

"Climbing down there. What's it look like?"

This deep into the forest, the ground was always a little wet, but it hadn't rained recently, so I still managed to find some decent handholds on the sheer surface.

"We've sent someone to fetch climbing equipment," another person called down after me.

"That'll take too long," I called back, keeping most of my focus on the placement of my hands and feet as I carefully climbed my way down. "This is faster. I'll go take a look and see if anyone needs help. Make sure someone calls emergency services."

I'd scaled plenty of tall cliffs before, and often without proper climbing gear, but that had been in my youth when I was at the peak of fitness. This climb was harder than it should have been, and as I felt the strain in my arms and legs, I vowed to double my usual workout time.

I was running before my feet even hit the ground. The fallen tree and the smashed tent were farther away than it had seemed from the top of the cliff, but the distance practically disappeared under my feet, and I was soon kneeling beside the wreckage.

There wasn't much left of the tent. It was just a mess of broken poles and ripped canvas. I riffled through what little I was able to reach but didn't see any evidence of a body.

My relief was short lived.

Near the top of the fallen tree, a leg was just visible between the branches.

I cursed again and pulled the knife from my belt to start cutting away the smaller branches in order to see what I was working with.

Ordinarily, we'd trim more of the branches from the trunk of a tree we intended to cut, but we'd been rushing, and some of the preparation steps had been skipped. I wasn't even sure who to blame.

The higher-ups for rushing us?

The person running the rig that had cut the tree?

Mostly, I blamed myself. I should have put up more of a fight against the impossible orders we were given. I should have insisted that we start on the south side of the area, where it would be safer to work, and double checked that all safety measures were being followed to the letter.

I wasn't the manager. Assuring these things wasn't my job, but that would be little comfort to the person who'd been hurt.

Or worse.

I'd seen dead bodies before. I'd even seen the bodies of people I'd killed with my own hands, but it never got easier.

I never let it get easier.

While in the military, I'd come across people who'd been fighting so long that death no longer bothered them. They could pull a trigger and take a life without blinking an eye. They treated the act of killing with the same casual indifference as sharpening a pencil.

I would never be the same.

Even as I specialized as a sniper and racked up a kill counter higher than most, I remembered every face and regularly recited every name I knew.

That was all supposed to be done. I wasn't supposed to add any more names to that list.

I managed to clear away enough of the branches to get a proper look at the victim. The man was lying on his front, so I couldn't see his face, but his chest was moving.

He was breathing.

He was alive.

My first instinct was to immediately

roll him over and pull him away from danger, but I stopped myself. The person had dodged out of the way in time to avoid the trunk of the tree, but he'd still been hit with the branches. He was probably injured, and suddenly moving him would just hurt him more.

Still, I couldn't leave him face down in the mud.

I'd received some basic first-aid training during my time of service, and it came in handy now as I delicately rolled him over in a way that kept his head and spine supported. There were no obvious signs of injury other than a cut on his scalp and even that wound didn't bleed much. Someone could easily be tricked into thinking that he was fine, and the sluggishly bleeding cut was harmless, but I knew from experience that unseen injuries could be the worst. The man had been hit by a falling tree. There was no way he was fine.

Shouting from above caught my attention. The others had managed to find some climbing gear and were making their way down the cliff. Emergency services had been called, and a rescue crew was being sent out to retrieve the injured man.

He was a complete stranger to me, but as I wiped the mud off his face and checked his breathing again, I was overwhelmed by a wave of protectiveness that I typically only felt for Magnus and Creed.

"You're not alone," I assured him. He was unconscious and probably couldn't hear me, but I couldn't help offering him comfort anyway. "Help is on its way. Everything's going to be all right."

***

Everything was not all right.

Emergency services had taken the man away in a rescue helicopter and transported him to the nearest hospital. Emberwood wasn't large enough to have a hospital, only a local clinic, but luckily our work site was relatively close to the town of Rynkirk, which did have a hospital. To most of the world Rynkirk would probably seem like a small town, but compared to Emberwood, which only had a single stoplight, it was practically a city.

Once the unconscious man was taken away, the rest of my coworkers considered their role in the incident over, and everyone went back to work. The area where the tree had crushed the man's tent had been roped off to be investigated later, but otherwise everyone was happy to forget that the whole disaster ever happened.

I returned to work as well, but I couldn't get thoughts of the injured man out of my mind. So, when my shift ended, I drove out to Rynkirk to visit the man in the hospital.

I didn't even know who to ask for, since I didn't know the man's name, but as soon as I explained the situation to the nurse at the front desk, I was ushered through the doors with surprising urgency.

The man had been given a private room, and a doctor was standing over the bed scowling down at a clipboard. She greeted me when I stepped through the door, barely listening to my explanation about who I was before grilling me about the man in the bed.

"Anything you can tell us will be helpful. We're having trouble identifying our John Doe here, which makes treating him harder."

"Oh." I twisted my hands together. Usually, I felt like the largest person in the room, but under the unforgiving florescent lights and the doctor's scrutinizing eye, I felt unnaturally small.

"I was the one who reached him first, but I don't know much more than that. He had a tent set up, so he'd probably been out in the forest for a while, but there wasn't anything indicating his identity. Is there a problem with his injuries?"

The doctor sighed, pushing her glasses up out of the way to rub at the bridge of her nose. "No. He's in surprisingly good condition after having a tree fall on him. He must have dived out of the way in time to avoid a serious blow. I want to say that he'll be fine once he wakes up, but without knowing his medical history, we have no way to know for sure. I'm hesitant to even prescribe basic painkillers. For all we know, he could be allergic, or taking other medications that might have an adverse effect."

"I see." My voice trailed off quietly as I glanced at the man in the bed. He'd been cleaned up since I saw him last, so his features were easier to discern. He seemed to be about my age, maybe a little younger, with curly brown hair and olive toned skin. The structure of his face implied some Greek heritage, and at least a few days' worth of dark stubble shaded his jaw.

The white bandage wrapped around his head stood out starkly against his hair and skin, but other than that, he looked like he was merely sleeping.

Looking at him, my mind raced at a million miles an hour. Nearly half a day had passed since I found him. If authorities still couldn't identify him, it meant that no "Missing Persons" report had been filed. Even if he had people in his life who cared about him, they weren't looking for him yet.

If I went missing for half a day, Magnus would be tearing the mountainside apart by now looking for me, and Creed would probably abandon his latest mission overseas to join the search. I didn't have a lot in life, but I had people to miss me. It was easy to forget how precious it was to be missed.

I wanted to ask if I could stay with the man for a while, even though I wasn't family. The idea of him lying in a hospital bed completely alone didn't sit right with me, and I figured my presence couldn't hurt anything. However, before I got the chance to ask, the machines around the room started to beep and the man on the bed woke up.

His eyes sprang open like they were attached to springs, but he continued to lie perfectly still. The hazel eyes behind his lids were dull and blurry, like he wasn't fully awake, and it took several moments for his pupils to focus.

Neither the doctor nor I made a sound as we waited for his reaction.

His eyes moved first, his gaze darting around the room. Then he tried to sit up in a single sudden motion. He didn't get more than a few inches off the bed before his injuries caught up with him and he grasped his bandaged head with a gasp of pain.

"Sir, please don't get up yet," the doctor spoke up, placing a hand on his shoulder to keep him still. "Just relax and I'll raise the bed up. Now, can you tell me your name?"

The bed adjusted slowly with the hum of a struggling motor. When the man was finally sitting up, he couldn't seem to decide what to look at first. His head swiveled back and forth on his neck, trying to take in the entire room all at once. It took two more attempts from the doctor to ask his name before he finally realized someone was speaking to him.

"Uh, Ellis. I'm Ellis."

"Okay Mister... Ellis." The doctor kept her tone light, but her brow was furrowed with worry. "You're in Rynkirk General Hospital. You were brought here after you were injured while you were camping. Can you tell us anything about what happened?"

The man, Ellis, shook his head back and forth. "I don't know."

Something about his tone sent a rock sinking into the pit of my stomach.

The doctor took his pulse and listened to his breathing with her stethoscope, never letting her professional demeanor drop. "Okay, sir. I understand that you're confused. Let's start with something simpler. We didn't find any ID on you. Can you give us your full name for our records?"

"I don't know."

His voice was sharp and panicked as he dropped his head into his hands, fingers digging into the pristine white bandages on his forehead.

"I don't know. I don't know. I don't know."

CHAPTER TWO

Ellis

A LIGHT FILLED my vision, and my eyes watered as I struggled not to blink. The light came and went quickly, and a moment later the doctor was stepping back from where she'd been leaning close to me.

It wasn't the first time she'd examined me. Not even the tenth time by now. Yet, despite all the examination and testing, the diagnosis never changed.

Amnesia.

That single word summed up a complex diagnosis. Apparently, I'd been camping in an area of the forest where a logging company had been working, and a tree had fallen on me. Why I was camping in a restricted area, or how long I'd been there, no one could tell me.

They couldn't even tell me my full name. There'd been no identification on my body, and so far authorities hadn't been able to track down any clues as to my identity.

My name was Ellis. That much I knew, but I wasn't even sure if that was my first name or last. The rest of my mind was completely blank, with just that single word bouncing around in my otherwise empty skull.

"Well, Mister Ellis," the doctor said as she scribbled something on my chart. "You're doing well. The swelling in your brain has gone down, and the cut on your head is healing nicely. No signs of infection or other symptoms. If not for the amnesia, you're practically in perfect health."

"Other than the amnesia," I repeated, unable to keep myself from scoffing.

"Yes," she nodded in understanding. "I understand that this must all be very confusing. Head injuries are tricky. Your memories may eventually come back, or they may not. You have a lot of factors in your favor, since you're in otherwise good health, so I have hope that the memory issues will resolve themselves, but all we can do for now is wait and see."

"Wait and see." I felt like a parrot, just repeating everything I heard. "Where am I supposed to do that? Am I staying here, or…"

I trailed off, not even sure what the rest of that statement would be. Surely I couldn't stay at the hospital. Hospitals were for sick or injured people, and as the doctor had said, I was mostly fine.

Was there a place for people with no memories to go?

I'd never heard of such a thing, but considering my lack of memory, maybe I'd forgotten about it.

Even a hotel was out of my reach. Hotels required money, and if I had any, I didn't remember how to access it. Without an identity, I had nothing. Even the clothes off my back weren't worth much. An attempt had been made to clean them up, but the incident with the tree had left them so stained and torn that I'd elected to stay in the hospital gown for as long as possible.

I literally had nothing.

I expected the doctor to give me more bad news, but to my surprise her voice suddenly brightened. "Actually, I think the answer to that question just walked through the door."

A moment later, a familiar figure stepped into the room.

BRODY

"Hey, you ready to go?"

Brody Stark had visited me several times since I woke up. Each visit was more awkward than the last.

What was I supposed to say to this stranger that had literally pulled me out of the mud?

Yet, at the same time, the sight of him also brought me a sense of security. He was the first thing I saw when I woke up. Maybe people with amnesia were similar to baby birds, and I'd imprinted on the first thing I saw, but some instinct inside me said that I could trust him. Everything else around me felt foreign and hostile, but this large redheaded man was an island of safety.

Oh, wait. He'd asked me a question.

What was it?

I'd been too busy staring at him and completely forgot what he said.

"Um... sorry. What?"

Rather than get upset, he simply

laughed and repeated himself.

"Are you ready to go. I brought you some clothes since yours were destroyed. I hope they fit."

"Clothes?"

I really wasn't doing much to break the parrot imagery as I continued to repeat everything that was said to me. There was so much I wanted to say, so many questions I wanted to ask, yet the words wouldn't come.

"Oh." Blue-green eyes stared at me, wide with concern. "Have they not told you yet?"

This finally gave me a question I could actually ask, but before I managed to say anything, the doctor spoke up instead.

"I was just getting to that. Mister Ellis, since your injuries are otherwise fine, you'll be discharged from the hospital soon. The authorities are still trying to identify you, so in the meantime Mister Stark here has offered to let you stay with him.”

Offered?

The doctor said that as though I had any other choice.

I gave some vague words of agreement, and before I knew it, I’d been discharged from the hospital and shuffled off into an unfamiliar truck.

Brody sat behind the wheel, keeping his gaze on the road as he explained that he didn’t live in Rynkirk, but in the next town over called Emberwood, so we would have a little bit of a drive to reach his home. His words washed over me like waves smoothing over an already clear beach, barely creating a ripple. I was completely detached from my body, as though I were floating a few feet above myself and watching everything from a third person perspective. It was all meaningless. I couldn’t even drum up the energy to feel nervous.

My heart was as blank as my head.

Without memories or emotions, did I even count as a person, or was I just a doll pretending to be human?

A sudden touch against my arm jolted me out of my thoughts. We were stopped at a red light, and Brody had placed a hand on my shoulder, but when I flinched, he immediately withdrew back to his side of the truck.

"Sorry. I didn't mean to scare you. I'm sure this is all very overwhelming. You just seemed upset."

"I'm not upset," I shook my head. "I'm not... well, I'm not anything really. I don't know. Everything feels so distant. I should be grateful that you're taking me in. I *am* grateful. I just... don't know what to say."

The light turned green, but the car didn't budge as Brody continued looking at me instead.

"You don't have to say anything. Hell, it was my crew that dropped a tree on you. I should be the one apologizing. Letting you stay with me is the least I can do."

The person in the car behind us pressed on their horn, holding it down so the blaring sound rang out through the otherwise empty intersection.

I jumped and covered my ears against the noise, but Brody just sighed and gestured into his rearview mirror.

"Don't get your panties in a twist. You're not gonna die if you have to wait a few seconds. Go around if you're that impatient. Not like there's anyone coming, anyway."

He said this, but he still pulled the truck forward anyway. As soon as we started moving, the driver behind us swerved around to cut in front of us. As they passed by, they flipped Brody a middle finger before speeding off with a squeal of tires.

I gripped tight to the handle of the

door. The sudden loud noises were irritating, but even worse was the thought that the person in the other car was mad at us. Just thinking about it caused my heart rate to spike and I had to take several deep breaths.

"You okay?" Brody asked when he noticed my reaction.

"Fine," I said, and I almost managed to keep my voice steady. "It's just strange being out here after spending several days in the hospital.

"Well, I can't promise my place will be quiet, but we can at least give you something better than hospital food."

This did manage to get a laugh out of me, albeit a very small one, until I realized that I didn't even know my own favorite food.

Was it pasta of some sort?

Maybe lasagna?

Maybe. I was pretty sure noodles were involved somehow. Thinking about various types of Italian food made my stomach flip with hunger, but that might have just been a result of the crappy hospital food I'd eaten for the last few days. Any proper food sounded like my favorite thing right now.

I spent the next several minutes listing every different type of food I could think of in my head.

How strange that I could identify all these different foods, and even recall what they tasted like, but I couldn't remember which ones I preferred.

As we kept driving, Brody filled the silence telling me about his home in Emberwood. He was retired from the military, and it was a shared homestead that he was in the process of building with his other veteran buddies.

Out of the corner of my eye, I gave Brody a closer look. When I thought about the concept of retirement, the picture that came to mind was of someone in their later years of life. Seventies or maybe even eighties. Brody, on the other hand, seemed to be about my age. At forty-five I wasn't exactly young, but I wasn't retirement age, either.

At least, I didn't think so. Without knowing what I did for a living, I couldn't be sure.

Either way, Brody didn't fit the image of a retiree, and hearing such a word from his mouth felt wrong. He was a large man, full of life and vigor. Nothing as depressing as retirement should be part of his description.

The description of his home lasted until we reached the edge of town. As soon as we crossed the border out of Rynkirk, trees practically seemed to spring up around us, blocking our view of the town behind us. If I didn't know Rynkirk was only just down the road, I would have thought we were lost in the middle of nowhere. The forest around us was mostly untouched by man, practically the same now as it had been hundreds of years ago. Even in the middle of the day, the trees shaded the road and made everything look like perpetual twilight.

What had possessed me to go camping alone in the middle of such a landscape?

I couldn't imagine doing such a thing now. Either, I'd turned into an entirely different person when I lost my memories, or my past self had a very important reason for being out in that tent.

We'd barely left Rynkirk behind when another car pulled up behind us. There was only one road leading out of town in this direction, so the presence of another car wasn't suspicious and didn't deserve any special attention. The only reason I even noticed the car was because it didn't have its running lights on despite how dim it was under the trees' heavy canopy. Sure, it wasn't nighttime, but in such low lighting having their lights on would still be safer.

Then, shortly after the car appeared behind us, Brody brought our truck to a sudden stop. A tree lay across the road, completely blocking our path. We had no choice but to come to a stop, along with the car behind us, and both vehicles were left idling in the middle of the road.

"Now what?" I asked Brody. "Should we call someone? Let them know that a tree has fallen down here."

Brody didn't look at me. His hands gripped tight to the steering wheel as he glared at the tree.

"It didn't fall."

"What?"

"That tree didn't fall," he repeated. "I'm a lumberjack. I know what a fallen tree looks like. There's no disturbed earth where the tree roots pulled up. It didn't just fall. It was placed there."

Grabbing the stick shift, he put the car in reverse, but when he looked in the rearview mirror, he froze.

I turned in my seat to see what had caught his attention behind us, and nearly had a heart attack.

Several men climbed out of the other car, each wearing a mask that covered their face, and several of them holding weapons. It looked like something I'd seen one of the movies I'd watched while waiting in the hospital and I almost suspected I was dreaming.

Except I wasn't dreaming.

I dug my fingers into the truck's leather seat hard enough to make my nails hurt, and the pain made it very clear that I wasn't dreaming.

Brody's hand squeezed my shoulder.

"Wait here. I'll be right back."

Before I could say anything, he reached into the backseat of the truck and pulled out a surprisingly large gun. The sight of it left me speechless as my mouth gaped like a fish, yet he held the weapon with a casual kind of ease as he opened the door.

In one fluid motion, Brody stepped out of the truck, braced the gun against his shoulder and pulled the trigger. I was almost certain that I'd never heard a gun in real life, because I was surprised by the noise it made. In movies, gunshots had a deep resonant sound, but the one in Brody's hands made a shallow popping noise.

I was so surprised by the unexpected sound, that for a moment I forgot to be scared.

One of the masked men dropped to their knees, clutching their leg where a patch of red quickly spread over their thigh.

"That was a warning," Brody shouted without lowering the gun or even removing his finger from the trigger. "Next shot is going between your eyes."

Like a cliché Mexican standoff, Brody

and the masked men stared each other down, none of them even daring to blink.

Right. Brody was retired from the military. I'd been so focused on the word "retired" that I'd overlooked the whole "military" part of his explanation.

When he said he was a lumberjack, I believed him without question. He fit the stereotype of a lumberjack to a T, right down to the red flannel shirt. The image of a soldier, however, didn't fit him and I hadn't been able to picture him in that position.

Until now.

Seeing him standing there, unafraid as he faced multiple enemies with a gun in his hand, I could easily imagine him in the middle of a war zone.

It was a strange shift in perspective. His familiar face became a stranger to me all over again. A harsh noise echoed in my ears, and it took me several moments to realize it was the sound of me hyperventilating.

The door on my side of the car opened. An iron strong grip on my arm pulled me out of the car. I was half tangled in the seat belt and fell out of the seat. The ground rushed up at me, and I threw out my hands to keep from face planting in the dirt.

I managed to catch myself, but a sharp pain shot through my wrist, and I cried out.

A masked man stood over me, luckily without a gun, though he did have a baseball bat.

It was pathetic. If we were both on our feet, I would have been significantly taller than him. Brody and I were almost of a similar height, so how was he able to stand his ground with such confidence while I ended up beaten down in the mud.

Again.

The masked man raised the baseball bat, preparing to swing it down at me. I covered my head with my arms in a feeble attempt to protect myself.

Another gunshot rang out with its startling little pop. The man standing over me shouted and stumbled away. I looked up just in time to see a clear hole right through the man's wrist, before he gripped the wound tightly with his other hand. Blood gushed between his fingers and formed a small puddle under his feet just inches from where I kneeled on the ground.

Immediately following the gunshot, Brody slid across the hood of the truck Dukes of Hazard style. His feet landed right in front of me, putting himself between me and my attacker. The butt of his gun slammed into the masked man's face, creating a satisfying crunch as bone and cartilage broke.

Through it all, Brody didn't say a word. No snappy one-liners and jeering taunts like the hero in an action movie would usually make. No, Brody was completely focused with lethal intent. This violent side of him may have been a stranger to me, but I was quickly learning that this formidable soldier side of him was a source of safety and protection.

Blinded by the pain of a shattered wrist and face, the masked man that tried to grab me stumbled back to his friends. Brody tried to follow him but was stopped when another gunshot was fired. Our attackers had started firing back.

Rather than follow them, Brody ducked down behind the body of the truck, bringing me with him to ensure I was safe as well.

A few more bullets bounced off the truck as our assailants piled into their car and drove away back toward town. As their taillights disappeared into the gloom of the forest, my last sight of them was a clear view of the empty spot on the back of their car where their license plate should have been.

"Are you all right?"

My gaze snapped back to Brody, my eyes wide enough that I could feel air sneaking under my eyelids. My breathing was still rapid and shallow, though I'd managed to keep myself from having a complete panic attack.

In contrast, Brody was completely calm as he inspected my wrist.

"Does it hurt?" he kept asking. "You landed weird when they pulled you out of the car. I'm sorry. I wasn't focused enough. I never should have let anyone get that close."

My laughter sounded hysterical, even to my own ears. "Not focused enough? If you were any more focused, lasers would have been shooting out of your eyes. I'm the idiot who can't even defend himself against a baseball bat."

"Stop," Brody said, his voice hard. "Don't talk about yourself like that. You've already been through a lot, and most people wouldn't know what to do if they got jumped by a bunch of armed men in the middle of a deserted road."

His voice may have been harsh, but his hands were gentle as he carefully inspected my wrist.

"You knew what to do," I grumbled, though I obediently kept my hand held out for him to manipulate as he wanted. "You didn't even hesitate."

"That's different. I've had training. Your wrist seems okay. I'm not seeing any obvious injuries. How does it feel?"

I swiveled my wrist around on its joint. It was a little sore, but didn't seem to be broken or sprained.

"It's fine. But, now what are we going to do?"

When he looked at me with confusion, I nodded toward the tree that was still blocking the road.

"Ah, right," Brody said, as if he'd only

just remembered the obstructing tree existed. "Don't worry. I've got it."

Standing up, he jumped into the back of his truck. After rooting around in the truck's toolbox for a moment, he held up a whole chainsaw for me to see.

I wasn't sure what my face was doing, but whatever expression I made must have been hilarious, because Brody outright laughed at me.

"What? I'm a lumberjack. What else would I be carrying in the back of my truck? Give me a few minutes and I'll get that tree out of the way, then we can get out of here."

The chainsaw wasn't small. Most people would require two hands to support it, yet Brody easily carried it with one hand as if it weighed nothing. The muscles in his forearms bulged as he lined the chainsaw up with the side of the tree, and my throat suddenly felt dry.

Swallowing a few times, I had to look

away.

My gaze trailed idly over the ground and caught on the puddle of blood that my attacker had left behind. Sudden pain assaulted me, like a thin needle being inserted into my skull just above my left eye. The image of blood mixing with dirt hovered behind my closed eyes, shifting into a new but similar scene.

As the peace of the forest was broken by the sound of a chainsaw revving up, I continued to sit there in the dirt, marveling at the feeling of my first true memory filling my mind.

***

Brody's home wasn't what I expected. When he'd described the place, he made it sound like a typical house with a homegrown garden on the land.

Instead, what I discovered was a significant patch of land with multiple houses and buildings in various stages of construction and a garden large enough to be considered a small farm. The sun was going to set soon, and its last rays of light cast everything in a golden glow. It didn't look real, like something from a movie set rather than real life, and I stared out through the window at the scenery in awe.

The moment the truck came to a stop, even before Brody had shut off the ignition, two other people immediately approached us.

Magnus co-owned the property with Brody, and with his long blond hair, he honestly looked like something out of Norse mythology.

The second man, Trent was just as well built as both Magnus and Brody, though he lacked a certain edge that marked him as a military man. He didn't live on the property, but I got the feeling he was comfortable there. I was given a quick introduction, and was able to pick up that Trent was someone significant to Magnus.

Partner?

Boyfriend?

I was already feeling so overwhelmed that the exact title flew right past me. The drive from Rynkirk to Emberwood hadn't taken that long, even including our pit stop for an unwanted shootout. Yet, I was already exhausted.

Luckily, Brody noticed my flagging energy and herded me off into the guestroom of his own house where a shower and a fresh set of clothes waited for me. I'd once again managed to get completely filthy, so the shower was appreciated, but I felt odd about the clothes. They belonged to Brody, the inclusion of red flannel made that obvious, and while they fit me well enough to make do for now, they still weren't my own clothes.

I didn't have my own clothes. I didn't

have my own anything.

I was grateful for his help, but how long would it last?

If the authorities never figured out who I was and I never got my memories back, would Brody just keep supporting me forever?

Or worse, what if I did get my memories back, and it turned out I was a terrible person?

Sitting on the bed in the little guest room, dressed in only a towel, I stared down at the borrowed clothes in my hand as guilt bubbled in my stomach.

I hadn't told Brody about the memory I'd regained. It wasn't much. I still didn't know my full name or anything about myself, but it was something. Maybe even enough to help them identify me.

Yet, during the rest of our trip after the shootout, I'd kept the secret of my returned memory locked tightly behind my lips and pretended it didn't exist.

All the doctors and nurses had talked about the potential to regain my memory as a good thing, but there was no guarantee that my memories would be pleasant ones.

If the first memory I'd regained was any indication, it might be best if all the rest stayed forgotten.

Sighing to myself, I started getting dressed. Moping around in a borrowed bedroom, hesitating to put on borrowed clothes, wasn't going to solve anything.

A few minutes later, I came back downstairs where Brody and the two other men were sitting on the house's front porch. I could see them through the window, and stopped when I noticed the dogs lying at their feet. Two of their dogs were some sort of large breed. I couldn't remember the exact name of either breed, but they were very muscular and even had a few scars like they'd been in a fight before. These two didn't surprise me, as they seemed like typical guard dogs that someone like Brody would have.

What did surprise me was the comically small Chihuahua sitting in Brody's lap. As the men talked, the little dog would occasionally let out a high-pitched bark, like it was contributing to the conversation. Every time it did, the larger dogs would raise their heads like soldiers standing to attention on the order of their sergeant. Eventually, they would relax and put their heads back down, but a few minutes later the cycle would repeat. It was an odd, but endearing sight.

That seemed to sum up the entire home that Brody had built for himself.

Odd, but endearing.

I was about to open the front door and join them when I realized I could hear their voices through a crack in the partially open window. I heard my name and knew they were talking about me.

Eavesdropping was wrong, I knew this, but I couldn't help myself. Leaning my back against the wall so I remained out of sight, I listened in on them.

"Maybe bringing this Ellis guy here wasn't a good idea," Magnus said while leaning over the arm of his chair to scratch one of the larger dog's heads.

"What was I supposed to do?" Brody immediately replied. "We dropped a tree on the man. I couldn't just leave him at the hospital. He had nowhere to go."

"I'm not criticizing your generous heart, Brody. But the moment you left the hospital, you were immediately accosted by a group of men with guns."

The rocking chair creaked as Brody leaned back. "After everything that's happened, it's not really surprising. I'm just sorry about the bad timing. Ellis shouldn't be dragged into all this."

With my back against the wall, I could only see part of the view out the window.

Magnus looked off to the side at something beyond my line of sight, which I assumed must have been Trent as the other man spoke up a moment later.

"Well, Brody, are you sure those men were after *you*? Like you said, the timing was bad. Everything's been quiet for a while now. Then, as soon as this guy shows up, you get attacked. It's still unclear why he was camping in a restricted area of the woods. For all we know, he could be involved with everything that's happening."

I didn't need to see Brody to know what kind of expression he was making. His audible scoff spoke volumes.

"What? You think he's responsible for the body we found?"

The other two men immediately disagreed, but I never heard what they said.

My lungs constricted and I couldn't breathe. A sound like buzzing flies filled my mind, and the sharp metallic taste of panic coated my tongue.

It tasted suspiciously like blood.

Body?

Someone had found a body?

Immediately, my mind was filled with images of the shoot-out from earlier that day, and the memory of blood mixing with dirt.

White noise filled my mind, and I could think of only one thing.

Escape.

My limbs moved of their own accord, as if my body had switched over to autopilot. Brody's house wasn't particularly large. Even from my position by the front window, I could see straight through to the kitchen, including the door to the back yard. Beyond that door lay the rest of the property, and beyond the edge of the property lay a vast forest. If I was careful, no one would see me.

As quietly as I could, I moved away

BRODY

from the window and slipped out the backdoor into the shadows of dusk. Not a trace of my presence was left behind.

CHAPTER THREE

Brody

WHEN INDIGO AND Onyx stood from their places lying on the porch, I didn't think anything of it. The two dogs regularly patrolled the edge of our land, and it wasn't unusual for something to catch their attention around dusk, when all nocturnal creatures started coming out.

However, when Pip also ran off after them a moment later, I knew something was wrong. Once the little Chihuahua found a comfortable spot on someone's lap, even an earthquake wouldn't move him.

Sharing a look with Magnus, I signaled for him to stay put and followed after the dogs. It didn't take me long to find what had caught their attention.

"No. Stupid thing. Let go."

I hadn't known Ellis for long, but I still easily recognized his voice from a distance. I'd left him to get cleaned up in the guestroom, but following the sound of his voice, I found him a fair distance from the house, almost at the edge of our property. A few more steps and he would have disappeared into the tree line.

Onyx and Indigo each held onto one leg of his pants with their teeth, keeping him from going anywhere. His hands darted around, unwilling to hit either of the dogs, but unable to free the fabric from between their jaws.

Pip sat between Ellis and the darkness

of the forest as a last line of defense, calmly watching the scene unfold. His little ears perked up when he spotted me, but otherwise he didn't move a muscle.

"Going somewhere?" I asked as I approached.

Ellis jumped at the sound of my voice and he nearly tripped over the dogs that still held his legs in place. I grabbed his arm to keep him from falling and felt him flinch away from my hand.

"I was just..." he tried to say, but didn't even manage to finish the sentence.

There was an emotion in his eyes that hadn't been there before. Fear and uncertainty I expected.

Who wouldn't feel such things in his situation?

Now, however, he reminded me of a prey animal. Like some hunted creature that was trying to flee for its life.

I tightened my grip around his arm. "What's wrong?"

He didn't try to remove my hand, but he kept staring at it as if I would suddenly strike out and hit him. Biting my tongue, I swallowed down my annoyance.

"Look, if you want to leave then I won't stop you, but wandering off into the woods without any supplies is dangerous. You aren't even heading in the direction of town. There's nothing but wilderness that way. Just tell me what's going on and I'll take you somewhere safe if you really want to go."

For a moment, it looked like he might argue. I could practically see the words coming together in his mind. Yet, before he could utter a sound, it seemed as if something inside him suddenly deflated. Like a building whose last remaining support beam finally snapped under the weight, he practically collapsed to the ground in a slump. This man was nearly my same height, but still managed to look distressingly small as he pulled his knees up to his chest in a defensive posture.

Taking a seat next to him, I occupied myself by petting Onyx and Indigo, and letting Pip crawl into my lap, while I waited for Ellis to find the right words.

It took longer than I expected. Dusk passed and night fully settled around us before he finally spoke up.

"I remembered something."

"That's good," I started to say, but the look on his face brought me up short. "Right?"

Ellis shook his head, tangling his hands in his thick hair. "No. I don't know. It's not really clear, but I think... I think I remember burying someone."

This time it was my turn to sit in silence for a few moments. That certainly wasn't the revelation I was expecting, though I supposed in the grand scheme of things it could have been worse.

Burying someone was better than killing someone.

Although...

"They weren't alive, were they?"

The shocked and disgusted look on Ellis's face told me all I needed to know.

"What? No. I wouldn't... at least, I don't think I would. I remember the smell of blood mixing with soil, and the weight of a body in my arms, but I'm certain the body was dead. It wasn't moving. It must have been dead."

He was starting to ramble, getting lost in the details of his single memory.

I moved closer to him and wrapped an arm around his shoulders, urging him to calm down. I'd seen firsthand how memories could change when reviewed too many times. If he kept obsessing like this, he'd probably convince himself that the body he buried had been alive.

"It's all right," I said as gently as possible. "We'll figure it out. If you did bury someone, I'm sure you had a good reason. There's no point in jumping to conclusions until we know what happened."

In an unusual offer of comfort, Pip crawled into Ellis's lap. The little Chihuahua usually hated strangers, but he allowed Ellis to pet him and run fingers through his fur.

There was a reason dogs were often used as therapy animals, and I saw the proof right in front of me. Almost immediately, his breathing evened out and he calmed down.

"What, um..." His voice was so quiet I felt the vibration of his words more than I heard them. "What were you talking about earlier?"

"Earlier? You mean when I was out on the porch?"

He nodded, uncurling from his defensive posture a bit while also holding Pip closer to his chest. "I shouldn't have eavesdropped, but I heard you and the others talking about a body you found.

What, um, what was it?"

There was an almost audible click in my mind as the mystery of his sudden panic snapped into place. "Oh, no. Magnus and I did discover a body buried on our property recently, but I promise you, there's no way you were the one who buried it."

As succinctly as I could, I explained about the one hundred and twenty-five year old body we'd uncovered. I mostly stuck to the relevant details, skipping over the unsavory parts like the objects in the coffin that people were following over the secret mausoleum, and the fact that there seemed to be some sort of cult connected to the whole thing.

He must have guessed that I was leaving some things out. As he listened to my explanation, he opened his mouth several times as if to ask a question, but he always stopped himself, shook his head, and stayed quiet.

It was for the best. Ellis had enough on his plate now. He didn't need to be getting involved with our affairs.

The most important thing was that the body we'd found had died over a century ago, and presumably been buried not long after. There was no way that Ellis could have been involved.

"But what if I was?" Ellis whispered so he was nearly drowned out by the sound of the wind rustling through the trees. "Not with the body you found, obviously, but somewhere out there is a body that I buried. What if I did something bad? What if I killed them? Maybe losing my memories was a good thing. I don't want them back if it means remembering something horrible." This time, even Pip's comfort wasn't enough to keep him from getting worked up as he started shifting back and forth where he sat. "That's selfish of me. If I killed someone then I deserve to remember what I've done.

Maybe I should go back to the police. Turn myself in. If I really did hurt someone then I should be locked up."

He moved as if to stand up, like he was going to run off to the cops right that moment.

I acted on instinct and grabbed him by the back of the neck, forcing him to sit back down. Once he was seated again, I still didn't let go and continued to hold him by the neck, even going so far as shaking him a bit.

It was a ridiculous sight. This was a large man in his early forties, yet I was scruffing him as though he were a misbehaving kitten.

No matter how ridiculous, though, it worked. Almost as soon as I grabbed onto him, he immediately calmed down. He didn't even try to fight me as he slumped on the ground, clearly exhausted.

"Stop," I ordered him. "There's no use getting worked up. We don't know what happened, and your memory isn't reliable. You're just going to get yourself hurt running off into the dark, and that's not going to help anything."

When I was sure he wouldn't try running off again, I let him go. For a moment, I considered apologizing for handling him so roughly, but he wasn't complaining, and it had worked, so I kept my apology to myself.

Through it all, he'd still kept a gentle hold on Pip. The Chihuahua didn't even look startled as he continued to sit in the other man's lap, perfectly content.

Ellis gave the dog's fur a few strokes before turning to look at me.

"If I get my memories back, and it turns out that I did hurt someone, will you make sure I turn myself in?"

I doubted the situation would be so simple, but that wasn't what he wanted to hear right now. All he wanted was some reassurance, so I agreed.

"Yes. I'll drag you to the police myself if I must. But not until we know exactly what happened. For now, you need to get some rest. Come on. I'll take you back to the house."

It turned out that Ellis was more exhausted than he initially seemed. Even once we got him standing, he was unstable on his feet. I had to escort him all the way to the guest room and practically tuck him into bed like a child. He was asleep the moment his head touched the pillow, and to my surprise Pip chose to curl up on the bed next to him.

Looking down at the sleeping man, I sighed and ran a hand through my hair.

What had I gotten myself into?

Leaving the bedroom, I turned off the light and closed the door as quietly as possible. Near the front door to the house, I looked out the front window where Magnus and Trent were still sitting. This was exactly where Ellis had been standing earlier when he overheard us, but now I was the eavesdropper.

When I'd left, Magnus and Trent had each been occupying their own chairs, but now Trent had moved over so he was sitting on the arm of Magnus's chair. I wasn't worried about the furniture. Magnus and I were both on the hefty side, so I'd built all the furniture extra sturdy. Even if all three of us plus Creed piled onto the chair it would still be able to support us.

No, what brought me up short was the way Trent was leaning into Magnus's space so they could whisper intimately to each other.

In all the years I'd known Magnus, he hadn't dated many men, and those he had dated didn't last more than a few weeks at most. This was different. Trent had already lasted longer than any previous lover before and was slotting into

Magnus's life with an ease that said he'd probably be staying for a long time.

Maybe even forever.

I was happy for him. I was happy for both of them. While I hadn't known Trent that long, it was obvious that he'd been lonely before, and I knew for certain that Magnus had been itching to find a companion. The number of times I'd seen him make a fool of himself trying to talk to an attractive man was proof enough of that. If they found that companionship with each other, then I wished them all the luck and would welcome Trent into the life we were building with open arms.

Yet, that didn't stop the pinpricks of jealousy that assaulted me every time I saw them together. Unlike Magnus, I'd never really sought a long-term companion before. I already had him and Creed, my pseudo-brothers, along with some biological family scattered around the country. Whenever I needed attention of a less platonic type, there were places I could go to have that particular urge satiated. So, a romantic partner hadn't been on the top of my priority list.

Or even on the list at all, if I was honest.

Seeing Magnus and Trent now, however, made me rethink this stance. Despite everything happening, Magnus had smiled more in the last few weeks than he had in the previous year, and Trent was definitely to thank for that.

The two of them made a romantic relationship look easy, and I couldn't help wondering what it would be like if I found something like that for myself.

Not that I even knew where to start looking. I had a lot on my plate right now, building our home and dealing with fallout from the body we'd found. Plus, options in such a small mountain town were limited.

Once again, I pushed these feelings

down to deal with them later. It had become such a habit that I didn't even need to think about it as I put on a neutral expression and stepped out onto the porch.

Magnus and Trent immediately leaned away from each other, though Trent didn't move from his spot on the arm of Magnus's chair.

"Anything wrong?" Magnus asked. His hand casually rested on Trent's thigh.

I sat down in my own chair heavier than I intended.

"Not wrong, but... things with Ellis are more complicated than I expected."

Magnus—the annoying bastard—just smirked at me. "Oh, dropping a tree on a man, causing him to lose all his memories, and then taking him home with you isn't a straightforward situation? I'm shocked."

Snatching up an empty beer can that had been sitting by my chair, I tossed it at

Magnus's head. "Shut up. No one asked you for your opinion."

Magnus responded by flipping me the middle finger with the hand that wasn't glued to his boyfriend's leg.

Eventually, after several minutes of childish bickering, I explained about the memory that Ellis had regained and his subsequent panic attack.

After I'd finished, the three of us sat in silence for a few moments. Onyx and Indigo had rejoined us on the porch and taken their usual place asleep at our feet. Their heavy breathing punctuated the night air, joining the hum of insects and the whispering of the wind in a natural symphony.

"So," Trent eventually spoke up, breaking the hush that had fallen over us. "I hate to bring it up, but I have to ask. Do you think he killed someone?"

I longed to crack open another beer, but the cooler I kept on the porch was empty and I didn't feel like going all the way back into the house to get one. Instead, I simply laced my fingers together over my stomach and leaned back as far as I could in my chair.

"I don't know. His memory might not be accurate, and even if it is, there aren't a lot of details to go off of. Burying someone isn't the same as killing someone."

"Plus, even if he did kill someone..." Magnus shrugged. "Well, we know from personal experience that there are a lot of reasons to take a life. That doesn't mean he's a bad person."

"But we also can't assume he's innocent, either," I added, glancing back at the house where Ellis slept upstairs. "For now, I'm just going to let him rest. We'll come up with a better plan tomorrow. All we can do is take it one day at a time."

***

BRODY

The next day, bright and early, we were interrupted by an unexpected delivery. Before Ellis had even woken up, and I was still drinking my first cup of coffee, a man showed up on our doorstep from Rynkirk's police department to drop of what remained of Ellis's belongings. They'd kept the destroyed tent and other various supplies to try and figure out Ellis's identity, but when nothing was forthcoming, they were apparently legally required to hand the items over.

I wouldn't have minded, except that the delivery came without warning, and the man making the delivery barely waited for confirmation that Ellis was here before dropping everything on my front porch and immediately leaving without another word.

Granted, a bunch of mostly broken items were barely worth the effort of delivering, so I could understand the man's frustration, but now I was left with a pile of useless junk blocking my front door.

Or maybe not so useless after all.

Magnus and Trent were still over at Magnus's house—and I was not going to interrupt them—so I was left to clear off my porch by myself. As I was sorting through the heap, separating the items that were broken beyond repair from the ones that could be salvaged, an idea occurred to me.

At almost the exact same moment, the front door opened behind me.

"What's all this?" Ellis asked as he stood in the doorframe. Sleep still clung to his eyes, and his curly hair was adorably rumpled. My clothes were a little too big for him and my shirt had slid to the side to expose one shoulder. The scene he created was achingly domestic, and a rush of heat flooded my skin. I quickly turned away, hiding my undoubtedly red face and cursing my pale complexion that showed off the slightest change in color.

"It's, um... the police came by and dropped off your stuff."

"Oh." Ellis's knees echoed against the wooden floor when he dropped down next to me and picked up the nearest item. It was an electric lantern, often used by campers, but the glass sides had been smashed to pieces and only the metal frame remained. "So, all this is mine?"

"Yeah." I took the lantern from his hands and placed it in the 'salvage' pile. The wiring still looked good, so it could probably be fixed. "The police were looking for anything that could identify you, but so far, no luck."

Ellis's gaze darted around at the various items, his eyes showing no obvious signs of recognition. "I see. Sorry to have all this useless stuff dumped on you."

He balled his hands into fists on his

knees, gripping his pants hard enough that he was in danger of tearing the fabric.

Reaching out, I placed my hand over his. "It may not be useless. Do you notice anything strange about all this stuff?"

At my implied request, he looked over the items again but shook his head. "No. Everything looks like standard camping stuff, I think. It's all broken, but that's not surprising."

"It's all new." I picked up the canvas from the tent and held it up for him to see. "It's hard to tell because of the damage, but most of this stuff has barely been used. There's no wear-and-tear like you would find on these items from general use. Like here. On this tent. Look past the bigger damage and you can see creases in the fabric like it was just pulled out of its package for the first time. Hell, some of this stuff still has price tags on it."

I handed him one of the items in question, a water bottle that was mostly undamaged with a price tag clearly stuck to its side. The sticker hadn't even started peeling yet.

Ellis turned it over in his hands, exploring it with his fingers as much as his eyes as if his identity might be written on it in brail. When he found nothing, he put it down and his gaze immediately gravitated back to me.

"So, does this mean something?"

The weight of his stare pressed down on me. Without meaning to, I'd become his compass. His north star guiding him through things when he knew nothing else and where he naturally looked for answers. The responsibility hit me all at once. I could tell him anything right now and he would believe me. Any order I gave, he would follow.

It was a heady sense of power, but also terrifying.

I couldn't meet his eye for long.

"It's a clue we can use to start looking for your identity. Assuming this is everything, and the police didn't loose part of it, then the supplies you had here would have only lasted for a few days. Based on where we found you, only Emberwood and Rynkirk are close enough for you to have hiked from in a few days. You didn't come through Emberwood. The town is so small that the appearance of any stranger would have been noticed. So, you must have passed through Rynkirk at some point. We'll visit the camping supply stores there and see if that's where you bought this stuff. Maybe someone will recognize you."

He nodded. It was a short, straightforward gesture like he wasn't even aware that he had done it. "All right. Do we go now, or..."

The sound of his stomach growling cut him off. He blushed and pressed both hands over his stomach to silence it.

I laughed and stood up, offering him a hand to help him off the floor. "How about we get breakfast first. Then we'll worry about what to do next."

Giving me another of those automatic nods, he grabbed my hand and didn't let go until we were in the kitchen where I deposited him at the table.

"All right. I just went grocery shopping, so we've got plenty of options. What do you want?"

I searched through the refrigerator for a moment, reviewing our options, until I realized he never answered me. A heavy silence hung behind me, and I cautiously peered over the refrigerator door.

Ellis sat at the table, staring down at his clasped hands with a pensive look on his face.

"You all right?" I asked.

He jumped and his knee hit the table, knocking over the salt and pepper shakers sitting there.

"Oh, sorry." He rushed to clean up the mess he'd made. "It's nothing. Anything is fine. Don't worry about me."

When he picked up the fallen shakers, he sprinkled some salt over his shoulder before putting them back in their stand. The gesture was so smooth, it was clear he hadn't even thought about it. Only once both shakers were back in their place did he realize what he'd done and stared down at the salt dusting his shoulder in shock.

"I don't know why I did that."

"Knocking over the salt is bad luck," I explained. "Tossing salt over your shoulder keeps the devil away."

He nodded again with his gaze still locked on his own shoulder. "That seems right. When I knocked over the salt, I had this overwhelming feeling that something bad was coming for me."

After brushing the salt from his

shoulder, he finally looked back at me with a wide searching gaze.

"I just acted without thinking. So, it must be something I do a lot. That means I must be superstitious, right? But I don't know why. Did something happen to make me superstitious or is it just an irrational belief." He nodded toward the refrigerator. "It's the same with food. I don't think I like eggs, but I don't know why. I don't even remember what they taste like, but at the hospital I always avoided them whenever they were served. It doesn't make sense."

Laughing quietly to myself, I pushed aside the carton of eggs I'd been about to take out and grabbed a packet of bacon instead.

"That could also be because hospital food is terrible. The eggs they serve aren't even real eggs. Avoiding them is just self-preservation. How about bacon? Do you have any automatic instincts about that?"

He shook his head, curly hair flopping into his eyes, and went back to studying the wood grain of the table while I started making breakfast.

It turned out to be a simple meal. Since Ellis was already confused about his own sense of taste, I didn't want to overwhelm him.

At first, Ellis just pushed the food around the plate with his fork, contemplating it more than actually eating. My first instinct was to insist that he eat. He was still healing from his recent head injury and his body needed fuel. However, I had to remind myself that I barely knew this man. Although I'd brought him into my home, we were still relative strangers to each other. Monitoring his eating habits would be going a bit too far.

Not even a quarter of his food was gone when he suddenly put his fork down.

"You don't have to do this, you know."

"Hmm?" I raised my eyebrows at him over the rim of my coffee cup. "Make you breakfast? That's what I do for most guests that stay at my house."

"No." He brushed his hair out of his eyes in frustration. "You don't need to help me so much. Earlier, when you were talking about visiting the camping supply shops, you kept saying 'we' like you just assumed you'd be coming along with me."

"Oh." I set my coffee mug down and pushed my mostly empty plate away so I could prop my elbow on the table. "I guess I just assumed... but I can see how that was overstepping. I'm sorry."

"No!"

In his haste to respond, Ellis's elbow accidentally knocked into his own glass, spilling orange juice everywhere. He cursed and jumped up from the table, snatching a roll of paper towels that was nearby to clean it up. I tried to help, but he shooed me away, leaving me no choice but to sit in awkward silence and watch him.

When everything was clean and he threw the soaked paper towels in the trash, he collapsed back into his chair at the table. Resting his head in his hands, he tangled his fingers in his hair and groaned.

"If it's not obvious, I'm pretty useless on my own. Can't even eat a meal without multiple catastrophes. Getting myself to Rynkirk feels impossible, let alone hunting down all the camping supply stores. I hate to say it, but I need help."

My coffee cup was empty. It was already my second cup of the day. I didn't need any more caffeine right now, but I really wanted it.

"So, what's the problem?"

Ellis slumped even farther in his seat, so his forehead was nearly touching the table. "I don't want you to feel like you have to help me. If I'm just some obligation to you then you'll eventually start to hate me, and I don't want that to happen."

Following my instincts, I placed a hand on the back of his neck. It had helped to calm him down when he was panicking last night, and this time was no different. Almost immediately the tension in his shoulders disappeared and he relaxed.

"You're not an obligation," I assured him, rubbing soothing little circles into the back of his neck. "I agreed to help you. That was my choice and I'm sticking to it. Once I agree to something, I don't half-ass it. I'm seeing this thing through till the end, and that means wherever you go or whatever you do, I'm going with you."

He sighed, and the last remaining tension disappeared from him. "If you say so."

Giving his neck one final squeeze, I let him go. "I do. Now, finish eating, then go upstairs and get changed into some proper clothes. Once you're ready, we'll head out and start our search. All right?"

Once again, he gave an automatic nod, and seemed to find comfort in the fact that he didn't have to think about his response.

Then he picked up his fork.

CHAPTER FOUR

Ellis

THE DRIVE OUT to Rynkirk felt both longer and shorter than I recalled. When I looked at the mileage, it was less than fifty miles. Yet, it also felt like we were traveling to the other side of the country. There was only one road connecting Emberwood to Rynkirk, and just yesterday, we'd been attacked on this very same road.

I was constantly on the edge of my seat, repeatedly checking the rearview mirror for any sign of someone driving up behind us. Every minute that passed seemed to take an hour, and I was immensely glad when we passed the boundary line for Rynkirk and left the tunnel of densely packed trees behind.

By definition, Rynkirk was a small town, but with a population of twenty-four hundred, that was still more people than we could question on our own. There was a very good chance we'd never find someone who knew me. I watched the pedestrians passing by on the sidewalk and wondered if any of them held the secret to my identity.

Brody brought the truck to a stop at a seemingly random spot on the road, and I realized I had no idea where we were going. I hadn't even thought to ask, and just trusted him to take me where I needed to go. Not for the first time, I was glad that he had taken charge. My brain felt so scattered and I hadn't even thought to look up a list of camping supply stores in the city.

Apparently, hiking and camping was a big tourist draw, and generated enough income that the town had three different supply stores. The first one we stopped at, *Nature Unlimited*, was the largest one. It took up an entire building on its own, which had been designed to look like a modern log cabin. A full taxidermy deer stood in a window over the doorway, posed among fake greenery and a few other smaller animals to give the impression that it was still alive. The deer was obviously meant to be the focal point of the arrangement, but I barely gave the creature a passing glance before focusing on a small black and white bird sitting on a fake branch near the deer's antlers.

I stood staring up into the dead animal's glass eyes, and a shiver traveled up my spine.

By now it was becoming a habit that

whenever I didn't understand my own reaction, I turned to Brody for an explanation. At first, I'd been afraid that he would grow tired of my constant questions and random statements, but in less than a day I'd already become so comfortable with him that I didn't even hesitate before turning to him and pointing above the door.

"Something about that bird bothers me."

He followed the line of my finger, and after studying the bird in question for a moment, a smirk spread across his mouth.

"I guess you really are superstitious. That's a magpie."

Magpies were a type of bird. I remembered that much, but not why the species was significant.

Noticing my confusion, Brody explained further. "There's an old superstition about the number of magpies. 'One for sorrow, two for mirth, three for a funeral, four for a birth.' There might be more to the saying that that, but that's all I remember."

"So, just one magpie is a bad sign."

Brody shrugged. "If you believe in that stuff."

It was clear I did. Even without my memories, the sight of the lone bird upset me.

Noticing my distress, Brody grabbed my hand and pulled me into the shop. "Come on. It'll be fine."

As we passed through the door, I automatically reached out and knocked on the doorframe three times. The sound of my knuckles rhythmically hitting against the wood soothed some of my worries, but I still clung tightly to Brody's hand.

The shop was busier than I expected inside. There were at least a dozen people, which wasn't a lot, but the narrow isles and fully stocked displays made everything feel cramped. Even with only twelve other people walking around, I felt like I had to keep my elbows pinned to my sides to avoid knocking into anyone.

I followed Brody right up to the front desk, where he rang the service bell to get the attention of the teenager sitting behind the register scrolling on their phone.

"What?" the girl asked without looking up.

At least, I thought it was a girl. The short blue hair, multiple piercings and tattoos, and all black attire made it hard to tell.

Maybe that was the point.

Non-binary was a thing, wasn't it?

Even with my memories, I had a feeling I wouldn't know the right thing to say in this situation, so I kept my mouth shut and let Brody do the talking.

To his credit, he didn't seem at all

phased by the cashier's attitude.

"Hi. I just need to ask you a question. Have you seen him before?" He pointed at me.

The abrupt non-sequitur question was enough to get the cashier's attention. She—they?—looked up from the phone and blinked owlishly at us.

"What?"

That must have been Brody's intention, for his smile just grew wider.

"I wanted to know if my friend had come in here recently to purchase anything, and if you or anyone who works here recognizes him?"

Still shocked by the unusual question, the cashier gave me a quick glance before shaking their head. "I don't recognize him. Let me see if anyone else does?"

After making a few calls and talking to the other staff at the shop, it was eventually determined that no one recognized me. If I had come to this shop,

I hadn't left enough of an impression to be memorable.

We left, disheartened but hopeful, and headed to the next shop.

It was the same at the next place as well. No one knew me. I should have expected as much. Being identified through my purchase at a camping supply shop was already a long shot, especially since we weren't certain I'd actually bought my supplies in this town.

"Come on," Brody said before I could get too lost in my own thoughts. "I think I saw a place selling barbecue nearby. Let's get some lunch before we do anything else."

The barbecue stand ended up being a pop-up food truck near a park. We got a couple of pulled pork sandwiches—meaning Brody bought them because I had no money—and we took the food over to a park bench where we could eat while watching the ducks.

"Sorry it's not a real restaurant," Brody said as he handed me one of the sandwiches. "I figured we didn't want to waste that much time. I'll owe you a proper meal later."

The sandwich was wrapped in greasy, wax-lined paper, which I had to carefully peel apart. "No. This is better, actually. There's more room outside. Is it just me or are all the places around here really small? I was constantly bumping into things at the shops we visited, and the restaurants didn't seem any better. Just looking through the windows, I could tell the booths would be narrow and uncomfortable. At least out here there's elbow room."

I waved my elbows around to show off the space around me, but realized the flapping gesture just made me look like a drunk duck, so I quickly stopped.

Brody laughed so hard he snorted. "This town isn't small. You're just too big."

I looked down at myself.

Too big?

Brody and I were similar in size, so I hadn't paid much attention to it, but thinking about it now, he was significantly taller than most of the people we passed.

Did that mean I was as well?

I didn't feel large. If anything, I felt too small, like there wasn't enough inside me to fill up a whole person.

"I didn't feel too big when I was at your place."

Huffing one last laugh, Brody took a bite of his sandwich before replying. "That's because Magnus and I are both on the large side as well. We built our homes from the ground up and designed everything to the scale that we wanted. It sucks, feeling like you don't fit into the world, so we wanted one place where we could always be comfortable."

Copying him, I took a bite of my own sandwich. Logically, I knew it was good. A heavy scent of spices reached my nose, but the food just tasted like ash on my tongue.

"So, you and Magnus are close?"

I hadn't asked about his relationship with the other man before. When I'd first arrived at Brody's home, I'd been too tired to pay attention to the other people around me. It was only now, with more energy and a clearer head, that I realized how unusual it was for two men to build a home together. It seemed like Magnus had his own house, and might even have a partner, but that didn't rule out the possibility of their relationship being romantic in nature.

It shouldn't matter to me. Brody was free to date or marry whoever he wanted, but for some reason I couldn't get the thought out of my head.

For the first time since we'd met, Brody

wasn't immediately aware of my discomfort as he kept talking.

"Oh, yeah. Known him for years. We met in the early days of our service, and just clicked, you know."

"Service?"

I hated how small my voice sounded.

Too large?

Bullshit.

I was nothing but a scared mouse walking around in the body of a bear.

The old, weathered wood of the bench creaked when Brody leaned back.

"Oh, right. I haven't told you about that. Magnus and I are both retired from the military. Risking your lives together certainly forms a bond, let me tell you. Actually, the fact that we're both on the large size is how we initially met. Due to the alphabetical line up, we were forced to share a bunk. That rickety old thing wasn't made to hold so much weight. It didn't last two nights before it collapsed on us. Magnus sprained his wrist and some of the broken metal gave me a good cut on my arm."

He held up his forearm to show off the jagged scar that reached from his elbow halfway to his wrist. What he classified as a "good cut" was probably what most people would consider a sizable wound.

Yet, he just laughed as he rolled his sleeve back down over his arm and carried on as if it were nothing. "That was an embarrassing report to write. I don't think our commanding officer would have believed us if the rest of the unit hadn't backed us up. They managed to find a couple spare cots, which they shoved in a corner for us. I think the cots were meant to be an emergency backup option, but they were actually more comfortable than the bunk beds."

"Uh huh." The sandwich in my hand was only half finished. I wasn't hungry anymore, but Brody had paid for it, so I forced myself to take another bite. My throat was dry, and I nearly choked while swallowing. "And, um, what made you decide to build a home together?"

"Oh, that was Creed's idea."

"Creed?"

Was that the other man I'd seen with Magnus?

I thought his name was Trent, but I could have been wrong.

"Yeah, Creed. I met him shortly after Magnus. The three of us have been a team for years. Decades at this point. His service isn't up yet, but he'll be joining us soon. He was the one who first figured out that we'd be able to afford a much better life after retirement if we pooled our resources, and the rest just fell into place after that."

I still had a lot of questions, like who the other man I'd seen with Magnus was, and what Creed thought about Brody bringing a stranger into their shared home. Yet, throughout Brody's entire explanation, there seemed to be no hint of romance between him and any of the others. I may not be the best judge of, well, anything right now, but surely a person's voice must change at least a little when they were speaking about a significant other.

That thought shouldn't have made me happy, and I quickly devoured the rest of my sandwich to try and drown out my guilt under the heavy taste of barbecue spices.

The last stop on our list was a small, out of the way supply store. It seemed like more of a local shop than something aimed at tourists. There wasn't even proper signage. Just a hand painted plaque on the front door that read *Big Martha's Place.*

A bell over the door rang when we entered. The sound was out of tune, and when I looked up, I could see that the bell was bent out of shape.

There weren't any other people, which made the shop feel larger despite being the smallest place we'd visited so far. Nothing on the shelves was labeled, and no matter how long I looked, I couldn't discern any sort of organization system. It looked like someone had merely dumped all the supplies on the shelves at once and never bothered to sort them out.

Off to one side of the shop, a middle-aged woman sat behind the register, reading a magazine that was at least ten years out of date. A nametag on her shirt labeled her as the shop's titular, Martha.

I'd gotten so used to Brody dragging me around, that I barely noticed when he grabbed my hand and led me over to the counter.

"Hello," he started to say, but was cut off before the first word finished leaving his mouth.

"I already told you before, no refunds,"

Martha grumbled behind her magazine.

"Excuse me?"

Stony eyes peered at me over the top of the glossy paper. "I told you when you bought the stuff. I don't do refunds. If you're here to complain, then you can turn right around and leave."

I nearly leapt over the counter and grabbed her, but self-preservation kicked in at the last moment and forced me to keep my hands to myself.

"You know me?"

The woman just stared at me like I was crazy.

Clearing his throat, Brody cut in between us. "Um, yes. Hi. This is kind of a strange situation, but if he really did visit here, then we'd appreciate it if you could tell us about it."

He explained what had happened to me as clearly as possible. It was obvious that she didn't believe him at first, but after I insisted as well, she seemed to come around to the idea.

"Amnesia. Well, fuck me, that's a new one." She tossed the magazine aside, which slid off the desk and landed on the floor somewhere out of sight. "Can't help you with a name, I'm afraid. You paid in cash, and didn't bother to introduce yourself. I can say that you seemed like you were in a hurry. Just demanded that I get you everything you'd need for about a week's worth of camping, shoved a wad of cash at me, then ran out the door before I could even give you your change. I only remembered you because of how bizarre it all was."

No name. No credit card. Nothing I could use to track down my identity.

Brody's hand tightened around mine. I couldn't remember when he'd picked up my hand again, or if I'd ever let it go in the first place, but I appreciated his support more than ever before.

"You said he ran off," Brody said. "Do

you know which way he went?"

"Yeah." Martha pointed behind her to the back of the shop. "He went off that way. I heard him run into my dumpster and wondered if he was lost. We're on the edge of town here and there's not much beyond this point. Just trees and a few walking paths out there."

It wasn't much, but it was at least something. Thanking the woman, we left the shop and headed around to the back of the building.

"Do you think this'll do us any good?" I asked when the dumpster was in view.

"Maybe," Brody shrugged. "If we can retrace your path, we may be able to find something to identify you. But even if we can't we at least know that our assumptions were correct. You were here. That's more than we had before."

There wasn't much space in the alley behind the two buildings, but just beyond the dense shadows I could see a green wall of trees waiting for us.

"Sure, but I'd still like—ack!"

While I was busy talking, my foot caught on a piece of loose concrete. I tripped forward and grabbed onto the edge of the dumpster to keep from slapping face first into the ground.

Laughing under his breath, Brody helped me back to my feet. "Well, at least we know why you ran into the dumpster." He pointed to a fresh dent in the side of the container right near where I'd grabbed onto it.

I barely heard him over the sound of ringing metal that echoed in my ears. The dumpster had made a particularly loud clang when I hit it. The noise bounced around inside my skull, knocking things loose wherever it went. I couldn't keep up with the vague images and impressions that flashed behind my eyes and gripped the sides of my head to silence the chaos.

Slowly, like a fading echo, everything

settled down, and a single picture was left behind.

"There was a tree." Grabbing onto Brody, I shook him in my excitement. "I remember a tree."

He wasn't as excited as I thought he would be. With this new revelation, I'd literally doubled my number of memories, but his face remained blank.

With one hand, he gestured toward the forest. "Uh, that doesn't really help us."

I scanned the forest near us, but none of them were the right tree. "No. There's a specific tree. It has pink flowers and a wonky branch. I remember it. Come on."

Dragging him with me, I headed for the tree line as quickly as I could without actually running. Just as Martha had said, a dirt hiking path split through the trees and disappeared around a bend after only a few dozen feet.

I started to move down the path but was suddenly jerked back by Brody's hand on my arm.

"Wait. You can't just go running off into the woods."

"But I came this way. I know I did. It's like... it's like a superstition. I feel it, even if I can't remember it."

Brody held onto me tighter. "I understand, but it's still not safe. We've managed to find this much. We can come back with supplies later."

"But..."

I hated arguing with him. Brody's words had become law in my mind, and disagreeing with him felt like committing a crime. Yet, I was so close to getting answers, I couldn't just turn away now.

"How about we just follow the path. I'm certain I stayed on the path, at least for a while. If it turns out I left the path, then we can turn back, but surely a hiking path would be safe to follow."

He sighed and pinched the bridge of his nose between his fingers, but after a moment he nodded.

"All right. We can follow the path for a while, but you're not setting one foot off the path, and if it starts getting too late, then we'll have to turn back whether we've found anything or not. Even a hiking path can be dangerous once it gets dark."

I probably would have agreed to anything at that moment if it meant we could keep following the trail of my memories. Luckily, Brody was only concerned with my safety and wasn't the kind of person to take advantage.

All of my clothing was borrowed from Brody, except for my footwear. Those were my one article of clothing that had survived the accident with the tree. The sturdy boots were well suited to navigating the dirt trail and supported the idea that I'd gone hiking off into the woods.

Now, if I could just figure out why I

had been out here, then maybe I could finally rest easy.

I hadn't told Brody this, but I'd remembered something other than a single tree. I remembered why the tree was important.

Something was buried beneath it.

Coupled with my memory of burying someone, I was afraid of what we might find, but I refused to turn back. One way or another, I needed answers.

As we followed the path, Brody told me about a few more stories from his time in the military. They were mostly funny stories, like the time Magnus had accidentally stepped on a hornet's nest and been chased around their base by a swarm of angry insects, and when they'd been posted in a foreign country that didn't speak much English and Creed almost accidentally got himself married to a girl from the local village due to a series of unfortunate mistranslations.

BRODY

I was certain that Brody was leaving out a lot of information from his stories, and maybe even completely making some of them up. Military service surely involved a lot more violence and danger, so he must have been cherry-picking only the most innocent events to tell me about. Still, I listened eagerly and soaked up every word he said like a desperately dry sponge.

Not once in any of his stories was there a hint of romance between him and the other men. Magnus and Creed were clearly important to him, possibly even closer than brothers, but it was an entirely platonic relationship.

It also turned out that Magnus was already dating someone. The third man I'd seen around their home was named Trent, as I'd thought, and although he didn't live on the property, he and Magnus had practically moved in together.

Brody completely supported the relationship despite it being between two men. While that didn't mean he was necessarily gay, it at least meant he accepted of homosexuality.

That meant there was a chance.

A chance for what?

I still wasn't sure, but I filed that information away for a closer examination later.

After a couple of hours of easy walking, the path began to tilt into a more drastic elevation. Soon enough, we were staring at an almost vertical cliff. It was traversable. There were obvious signs of people climbing it before, including several rungs that had been permanently hammered into the stone, but we wouldn't be able to scale it on our own.

"I thought as much," Brody said as he peered up at the top of the cliff. "Mountain terrain is treacherous even under the best conditions. A lot of hiking paths around here require some form of climbing gear to traverse. Well, it's good timing at least. We would have needed to turn back soon anyway in order to get back to town before nightfall."

"Uh huh," I nodded, though I wasn't really listening.

My mind was split into two places at once. I was here, with Brody, but at the same time I was also lost to the memory of facing the cliff wall for the first time. The two memories superimposed over each other until I couldn't differentiate between past and present.

A sense of urgency struck me, just short of true panic.

I needed to move. I needed to keep going or they would...

They would what?

It didn't matter. I had to keep going. The cliff required climbing gear, which I didn't have, so that only left me one option. I'd have to go around.

I looked left and right. To the right, the land angled downward. It wasn't steep, but it also wouldn't help me get past the cliff.

I'd have to go left.

Without warning, I darted off the path and into the trees, using the rock wall as my guide and sticking close to the cliff. Sticks and leaf litter crunched under my feet as I ran. I didn't know where I was going, yet at the same time it felt like a destination waited for me just ahead.

The sight of a particular rock formation brought my feet to a sudden stop. It looked no different than the rest of the rocks around me, but something about it filled me with fear. I could almost see someone appearing around the rock, lunging at me like they meant to attack. It was just a shadow, a figment of what was no longer there, but I reared back in fear all the same. My back hit the cliff wall, and I raised my arms to shield myself from an attack that never came.

It wasn't real. These were just memories of what had already happened. They couldn't hurt me.

The sound of approaching footsteps shattered my moment of clarity.

Someone was calling my name. They sounded angry. I really was being pursued.

Pushing off of the cliff wall, I kept running, this time heading straight into the forest away from the ominous rock formation. With each step I took, the air grew darker around me until the air under the forest canopy looked like dusk in the middle of the day. Small golden sunbeams occasionally broke through the leaves, illuminating roots and stones I needed to avoid. It was like the forest itself was spurring me on, helping me keep running and put space between me and my pursuers.

There was no telling how long I ran.

Minutes or hours, it all felt the same.

I began to grow tired. My breathing faltered and my steps slowed. I thought I was safe. I'd left my pursuers far behind and was safe within the labyrinth of the forest.

So, it was a surprise when, the moment I stopped running, something grabbed me from behind and forced me to my knees.

"What are you doing?" a familiar voice shouted in my ear. "Ellis. God damn it. You are the most self-destructive person I've ever met. Now answer me."

I knew that voice. That voice was safe. The hand gripping the back of my neck was also familiar, and although it should have been threatening, it only brought a feeling of safety.

"B... Brody?"

The moment I spoke, all the anger left his body, and he crushed me to his chest in a tight hug.

"Hey. It's all right. Whatever that memory was, it's over now. I'm sorry I yelled. You just scared me."

My cheek pressed against his chest and I automatically wrapped my arms around him to return the hug. Every inch of my body was shaking, and I panted so harshly I could taste blood. The scent of him, fresh cut cedar and bergamot aftershave, filled my nose and calmed my nerves with each breath.

"Someone was chasing me."

"That was me. I'm sorry I scared you, but I couldn't just let you run off alone."

"No, I mean..." I pulled back just enough to look up at him. "I remembered someone chasing me. Before. They were bad people. I was... I was afraid, so I just kept running. Being back here, it was so similar that I couldn't tell the difference between then and now."

Brody's arms around me tightened for a moment, before relaxing enough to let me pull away. "And I'm guessing that me chasing you at the same time didn't help."

"It did, actually."

I stood up. My legs were shaky, but they held my weight. The forest around us opened onto a small clearing. Among the patch of unobstructed sunlight, a single familiar tree stood alone.

"If you weren't chasing me, I wouldn't have come this far. I think... I think this is where I stopped after I got away the first time. Look. I know that tree. I've seen it before."

Small pink flowers and a wonky branch. It was exactly like I remembered.

I took a step toward the tree, but stopped and turned back to Brody, urging him to follow me. "I came into the forest to hide, but I was held up by the cliff. They caught up to me. The... bad people. I got away, but I decided it wasn't safe. I had to hide it."

Taking hold of my hand, Brody

followed me into the clearing.

"Hide what?"

"It's… something important."

At the roots of the tree sat a patch of freshly disturbed soil. Everything pointed toward the fact that something had been buried here, but right on the verge of getting my answers, I froze.

Before all this, I remembered burying someone. Surely whatever lay beneath our feet couldn't be a dead body.

Right?

I clearly remembered running here while being chased. I couldn't have done that while carrying the weight of a person, dead or alive.

Shaking away my worries, I knelt before the tree and started digging with my bare hands. The area of disturbed soil wasn't that big. Certainly not big enough to conceal a person.

Maybe my first memory had been wrong. Maybe I never buried anyone at all, and the memory had just gotten twisted in my mind.

Brody joined me, and together the two of us soon uncovered a small box.

It was plain, with no embellishments. There wasn't even a hinge. The lid just sat loosely on the top. I could easily hold the whole thing in one hand, and it barely weighed anything at all.

"Well," Brody nudged me. "Go on."

Taking a deep breath, I opened the box.

Inside, sat a key.

It wasn't secured by anything and rattled around loosely. Based on the sound alone, I could tell it was made from solid metal and seemed to be very old. About the size of my palm, it had intricate carvings on the handle and looked expertly crafted.

It also brought no memories at all. I remembered how desperately I'd run to get here, and how determined I'd been to hide the contents of this box, but when I looked at the key, I felt nothing.

This couldn't be it. There had to be more.

As I was still processing my lack of reaction, Brody suddenly snatched the key from the box. The little bit of metal looked ridiculously small in his large hands as he stared down at the key. His mouth hung open, and his eyes were so wide I could see the whites all the way around his blue-green irises.

"Where did you get this?"

All I could do was shake my head, gaping at him silently like a suffocating fish.

He waved the key in my face, pointing at the carving on the handle. "Do you know what this is? It's a poppy flower. This is Poppy Milford's key."

"Who's that?"

"It's—"

Before Brody could even begin to

explain, he was cut off by the jarring sound of his cellphone ringing. It was a miracle he could even get cellphone reception out here, but since he lived in these mountains, he probably had some way to ensure he always had a signal.

The sound of his ringtone made Brody jolt in surprise. Still gripping the key in one hand, he answered his phone with the other, putting it on speaker so he wouldn't have to hold it up to his ear.

"Magnus. What is it?"

"Brody," Magnus's voice rang clearly through the phone. "Whatever you're doing, you need to get back here now."

"Why? What's wrong?"

"Creed—" Magnus's voice broke and the phone suddenly went quiet.

Brody and I both checked the reception to make sure the call was still connected.

"Magnus," Brody shouted into the phone. "Talk to me. What about Creed?"

BRODY

Magnus's voice wavered, but he managed to spit out the words.

"I just got a call. Creed's gone missing."

CHAPTER FIVE

Brody

I HAD NO idea how I got home. One moment, I was staring at my phone in shock, listening to Magnus tell me that Creed had disappeared, and the next thing I knew, I was pulling my truck up the road back to my property. Everything in between was a blur.

Ellis sat in the passenger seat next to me, so I must have safely gotten him out of the woods and made the drive from Rynkirk to Emberwood, but for the life of me I couldn't have explained how I did it.

My body was completely on autopilot while my mind was a chaotic jumble of screaming and white noise.

Missing.

Not injured.

Not even dead.

Creed was *missing*.

Through all our years of service, the three of us had been through hell and back together. Faced every sort of danger, and supported each other through every sort of injury, but none of us had ever just disappeared. That was one security we always had. Even in the most hopeless situation, we at least knew where the others were.

Was there a word for "more than hopeless"?

A lack of hope meant there was space for hope in the first place. It was like the difference between a tree that had been cut down, and one that never grew. I couldn't feel hopeless about the situation because there was no chance for hope to grow in my heart in the first place.

No, I had plenty of feelings, all trying to get my attention at once, and none of them were empty.

The sound of the truck's door rang in my ears as I slammed it shut behind me. I vaguely registered the movement in my peripheral vision as Ellis slipped out from the cab of the truck.

"Magnus! What the hell is going on?" I bellowed.

I didn't need to shout. Magnus had come out of his house before I'd even touched my brakes, but it felt good to yell, nonetheless.

"I already told you on the phone," Magnus said as he approached, Trent trailing behind him and making his way over to Ellis. "Creed is missing."

In my blind drive back to Emberwood, I'd somehow managed to make pretty good time. The sun had only just set, and the soft edges of twilight hadn't yet given way to the true shadows of night. The lights glowing inside Magnus's house, and the bright porch light on my own home offered a comfortable invitation, promising warmth and safety. It would be so easy to just step inside my house, shut the door, and pretend nothing outside those walls existed.

I'd built those walls myself. I knew how strong they were.

A weaker man might have given in to the urge, but my feet stayed rooted to the ground outside as I demanded more answers from Magnus.

"I know you said Creed went missing, but how? What happened?"

Magnus ran his hands through his hair, pulling some of his long blond locks free from his braid. It couldn't even be called a braid at this point, as most of his hair fell in disarray around his face. He must have been pulling at it ever since getting the news about Creed. His frustration was obvious in the lines on his face.

"I got a call from some military official. You know the type. Sounds all official, but probably never leaves the safety of their desk. They said that Creed's unit was sent out on a mission, and he never came back. The rest of his unit is unharmed and were able to give a report. It seems like he was captured by someone."

"Who?"

I knew the answer just from the look on Magnus's face.

"Come on, Brody," he sighed. "You know how this works. Information like that is classified. If we were still enlisted, we might have been able to pry some more information out of them, but a couple of retired veterans..." He shook his head, and the last remains of his braid gave up. His hair tie fell to the ground and his hair was left hanging free. "We're lucky they at least respected Creed's emergency contact list and called us rather than Creed's family. If that happened, we'd probably never know anything was even wrong."

Magnus and I didn't have much family. I had a few relatives floating around the country, but none I was close with. Creed, however, did still have family. Creed never talked about them much, but what little he had shared made it obvious that things weren't great between them.

His family had expected him to move back home after he retired. We never did figure out how they learned that he planned to move to the mountain with us after his service was done, but they had been very unhappy about it. All three of us had been bombarded with calls for a week straight until we managed to block enough phone numbers to keep them at bay.

Magnus was right. If Creed's family had been the ones to learn of his disappearance, they never would have told us a thing about it. We would have continued our lives in ignorance until one day we tried to call him and couldn't get through.

"Fuck!"

I nearly kicked my truck in frustration. My foot even came off the ground, but I quickly put it back down after remembering all the work I'd put into restoring the old junker.

"Is there anything we can do?"

Magnus's only answer was to hold his hands out helplessly.

"Right. Of course not."

My legs were as supportive as overcooked spaghetti as I made my way over to my porch and sat down heavily on the front step.

Almost immediately, Indigo and Onyx

wormed their way under my arms, offering comfort in the only way a dog could.

Dust kicked up around me as Magnus's familiar boots stepped into view. "There must be something else."

I patted the dogs a few more times and looked up at him. "What're you mumbling about?"

The floorboards of the porch rattled under Magnus's weight as he sat down next to me. "There must be something else going on. Creed couldn't just get captured like that. How many missions have we been on? How many times have we escaped death without a scratch? Creed was always the most capable of us. He wouldn't just suddenly get captured."

Ordinarily, this would be the moment where I offered some form of comfort, or at least said something to snap Magnus out of his panic, but this time I had nothing positive to say.

BRODY

It all felt so inevitable, like I'd just been waiting for this moment, but now that it was here, I didn't know what to do.

"You're right. We have been on a lot of missions together. But maybe that's the problem. We've escaped death too many times. Sooner or later, it was going to catch up to us. Creed is the most capable, but even he isn't perfect. You know how it is. Mistakes are inevitable, and it only takes one for a mission to go off the rails. It sucks, but it's not our fault. All we can do now is hope that Creed manages to pull through whatever mess he's found himself in."

Before I even finished speaking, Magnus was already shaking his head, mumbling to himself. "No. No. No. It *is* our fault. We should've stayed."

He wasn't talking to anyone specifically, just putting words into the air. It wasn't even clear if he'd realized that he'd spoken aloud.

"We should've stayed with him. We could have found a way to extend our service for a few more months rather than retiring right away. Even if we couldn't go on active missions anymore, we could've at least helped him when he got in trouble instead of sitting here on our useless asses."

I sighed heavily, which caused Indigo to instinctively lick my face. "Maybe we could have, but that doesn't matter now. We're here, and Creed is God knows where."

Both dogs were startled and backed away when Magnus abruptly shot to his feet. "How can you be so calm?" Magnus shouted, pacing back and forth. It was a good thing Pip had decided to stay over by Trent and Ellis, or else the little dog would have been in danger of being stepped on. "Creed could be dead for all we know, and you're saying it doesn't matter. Fuck! Do you care at all?"

BRODY

He lashed out and kicked the railing surrounding my porch. I heard the sound of splintering wood but refused to take my gaze away from Magnus long enough to look at the damage.

His accusation hurt more than I was willing to admit. Taking advantage of the fact that I was a slight bit taller than Magnus, I raised myself to my full height, crossed my arms, and stared him down. "Is that really what you think of me? That I don't care? It was Creed's idea that we come here and start getting things set up first, and we agreed with him. There's no use regretting that decision now. So, stop freaking out. It's not helping anything."

Some of the poles from my porch railing must have fallen out, because Magnus kicked at something on the ground and there were more sounds of breaking wood.

"Well, one of us needs to have some reaction. It's better than your dismissal shrug. Fuck. Whatever. Do whatever you want. I'm gonna... I'm gonna... Agh!"

He stormed off, never finishing his sentence. Not that he could. There wasn't anything either of us could do and we both knew it.

The door to Magnus's house—which I'd managed to mostly finish building by now—slammed closed as he disappeared inside. Trent gave me a sympathetic look before following Magnus as well.

I finally looked over at my porch railing. It wasn't as bad as I feared. One of the railings was cracked and a few of the support poles were beyond saving. Overall, it wouldn't take more than a few hours of work to fix.

"If he's going to break something, he should take it out on his own stuff. Not mine," I growled. Sucking in another deep breath, I shook my head and headed around to the back of my house.

A shack behind my house held all my

woodworking tools. It was one of the first structures I'd completed after we bought the property, since I was going to need it to help build everything else. One entire wall was dedicated to my selection of high-quality timber. It took me a moment to search through the selection and find a few pieces of the same walnut wood that the porch was made from.

After building multiple structures, including two full houses, and a lifetime dabbling with woodworking, meaning that I didn't even need to think about what I was doing, my hands worked automatically, bringing the selected wood pieces over to the miter saw so I could cut them down to the exact size I needed.

"Brody?"

Ellis stood in the doorway to the workshop, halfway hidden around the frame as he peered inside. "Should you be doing that?"

"What?" I looked at him, confused as I

switched on the miter saw. "Yeah. I should fix the railing as soon as possible. It won't take long, and it'll bother me if leave it for later."

I placed the first piece of wood on the miter saw but was stopped when Ellis rushed inside and grabbed my wrist. "I don't think you should be doing that."

"Excuse me?"

Okay. Now I was starting to get upset. I'd built every structure on this property. Working with wood was literally my job.

Why was he questioning me?

My anger must have been clear on my face, because Ellis rushed to keep talking, never letting go of my wrist.

"I- I'm sure you're very good at this stuff. But, um, maybe not right now."

"What are you talking about?"

Tugging at me, Ellis tried to pull me away from the miter saw. "It's just... your hands."

"What about them?"

I looked down where Ellis was now holding both my wrists. My hands were shaking.

At first, I thought there was something wrong with my vision, but after blinking a few times I realized that, no, I wasn't seeing things wrong. My hands really were shaking. The walnut branch I held rattled against the table of the miter saw, completely unsteady. If I tried cutting it, I probably just end up sawing my hand in half instead.

I let go of the wood and it tumbled from my shaking fingers as I hunched down on the floor. I gripped my hands to my chest.

"Fuck. I just... fuck." No matter how hard I tried, I couldn't make the shaking stop.

Ellis carefully knelt in front of me. "It's okay. You're allowed to be upset."

"No. That's not..."

I shook my head against the pain that

was building between my temples. The buzz of the still running miter saw echoed painfully inside my skull and I slammed my fist against the power button to turn it off. I understood why Magnus had broken my porch railing. It felt good to hit something, and I slammed my fist against the button a few more times before Ellis stopped me and held both my hands in his own.

"Your friend's missing. Of course you're upset. And... your other friend, Magnus, is just upset, too. I'm sure he didn't mean what he said."

"What would you know about it?"

Ellis's face fell, and I immediately regretted my words.

"You're right. I don't know anything, do I. I'm probably wrong. I—"

"No," I interrupted him. "I'm sorry. I shouldn't have said that. You're right. Magnus is just upset. Of course he is. We've never been this helpless before.

There was always an enemy we could fight, or a scheme we could unravel. Even when we had no idea what was going on, we could always keep moving forward. Now... now there's just nothing. God! Even if I wanted to go looking for Creed myself, I can't. I don't even know what country he might be in."

The shaking in my hands increased, until my whole body trembled. All my thoughts were replaced with a loud buzzing sound, as if I'd turned the miter saw back on. Yet the saw remained silent. It was just my own brain going haywire.

Dropping my head into my hands, I pressed my hands to my ears trying to block everything out.

"Magnus is right. I am useless. Creed's going to die, and I'm just sitting here."

Arms wrapped around me. I didn't register the sensation at first, and when I did, I was too overwhelmed to question it. The arms held me just tight enough to help me feel grounded without smothering me, and I instinctively leaned into the embrace.

"It's okay," Ellis said over and over. "It's okay. It's going to be fine."

I barely heard him.

My chest hurt.

I couldn't breathe.

Somewhere in the back of my mind, I knew that I was hyperventilating, but I couldn't think straight enough to realize what it meant or what I should do about it.

A tug on the front of my shirt pulled me forward, and before I knew what was happening, lips pressed against mine. It wasn't the first time I'd been kissed, and I reacted to the sensation instinctively. Our mouths molded together, moving slowly, and soon, the pleasant friction and wet slide of a tongue against my lips was all I could think about.

The kiss didn't last long. After only a

few moments, Ellis pulled back and looked at me with a sheepish expression.

"Sorry. You were hyperventilating and I... I didn't know how to make you stop."

I merely blinked a few times, my thoughts as sluggish as if I'd gone days without sleep.

"You didn't know... So, you chose to kiss me?"

"I know, it was dumb," Ellis babbled, rocking back on his heels as he retreated from me even more. "I don't know what I was thinking. I just—"

I cut him off and grabbed his shirt to keep him from getting any farther away.

"It was a good choice."

Then, I pulled him forward and kissed him again, this time putting more force behind the action. His previous kiss had been chaste. A virgin on their first date could have stirred up more heat.

I aimed to show him what a kiss should really be like.

He gasped when I pressed against him, giving me the perfect opportunity to slip my tongue between his lips and deepen the kiss. I paused for a moment, waiting to see if he would protest, but after he got over his shock, he grabbed onto my shoulders and pulled us closer together.

In a move so smooth it was as if we'd practiced it, we moved together so Ellis was lying on the floor of the workshop, and I was kneeling over him. The kiss never broke, never even paused, and once I had him under me, I took full advantage of my new position.

I found his wrists with my hands, pinning them to the floor as I ravaged his mouth. He made the most wonderful sounds, gasping and moaning in response to everything I did. I slipped one of my legs between his, making him writhe when I rubbed my thigh against the prominent bulge of his arousal.

"Stop, stop," Ellis gasped when he

turned his head to wrench himself away from the kiss.

I froze.

"What's wrong?"

"I... I..." He was panting so hard he could barely get the words out, and his former olive complexion was bright red. "I'm about to... um, you know."

Glancing down, I saw the way his whole body trembled like a rubber band stretched to its limit. His arousal strained against his pants so desperately, I feared the zipper would burst.

Dipping my head down, I let my lips trail against his neck. "Sensitive?"

He whined deep in his throat and nodded.

Laughing under my breath, I nipped the skin right over his pulse point and watched him squirm.

Curiosity gripped me.

Was this sensitivity a result of his memory loss, or had he always been like this?

Even if his mind didn't recall his past sexual experiences, surely his body would still remember. Or maybe it really was an example of mind over matter. His brain couldn't recall any previous experiences, so his body reacted the same as a virgin.

Wait...

Following that line of thinking, could Ellis even consent?

Without memories to draw from, he may not even understand what he was agreeing to.

"Please." Ellis tugged at my shoulders. "Please, don't stop."

While wracked with indecision, I'd completely stopped moving. Ellis desperately writhed against me, wrapping one leg around my hips to bring our bodies closer.

Rather than listen to his demands, I sat up enough to look directly into his eyes.

"Please, what? What do you want?"

With his wrists still pinned to the floor, he shook his head back and forth. "I don't know. You. I just... want you."

"No." By moving his arms higher above his head, I was able to hold both his wrists in one hand. This left me a hand free to grip his chin and force him to look directly at me. "I need you to tell me specifically. What do you want?"

His other leg hooked around my hips as well, giving him leverage to grind against me.

"F... fuck me. Please."

His voice was small, and his face burned so brightly with embarrassment that it was practically a beacon in the night. Yet, his words were still unmistakably clear and there was no hesitation in his eyes.

Fuck it. I sighed to myself.

How could I deny such a direct invitation?

"All right." I pressed a quick kiss to his lips. "But not here."

Even if he wasn't truly a virgin, without his memories it wasn't that different. I'd be damned if I let his first remembered sexual experience happen on the dirty floor of my workshop.

Climbing to my feet, I took Ellis by the hand and guided him out of the workshop and inside the back door to my house. He followed me eagerly, clinging to my guiding hand as if afraid I would suddenly disappear. The distance from my workshop to my bedroom wasn't very long, but it still gave me enough time to think, and I didn't like where my thoughts were going.

This was a bad idea. For so many reasons. Forget about the ethical dilemma of sleeping with someone suffering from amnesia. This wasn't the time to get distracted by my own desires. Creed was missing, Magnus was upset, and we still had a whole mystery of a cult and an unidentified dead body to solve.

But damn it all, I was so tired of the constant worry. Just for one night, I wanted to forget about everything weighing on my mind.

Did that make me selfish?

Probably. But that was something that my future self could deal with. My current self was going to cast everything aside and indulge in one night of fun before reality slapped me upside the head in the morning.

I didn't bother turning on any lights. It was a full moon tonight, and the curtains were open, illuminating the room in a glow of silver.

My first instinct was to grab Ellis and pull his clothes off. Get down to business before I could second guess myself. However, as I started pulling at the buttons of his shirt, I stopped. We'd moved from the workshop to the bedroom specifically so Ellis could have a good first remembered experience. Acting like too much of a brute now would ruin everything.

Unless it turned out that's what he wanted.

Testing the waters, I carefully pushed him back until his legs hit the edge of the bed. Then, with slow gentle movements that he could easily pull away from if he wanted, I pressed forward just a little more. He tipped back and fell onto the bed, bouncing when he hit the mattress, so he landed in a disarrayed tangle of limbs.

"Brody?"

In contrast to his body, his voice was delightfully small as he looked up at me.

For the first time, I could admit to myself that, physically, Ellis was just my type. I'd always preferred partners that were a similar size as me. It meant I didn't have to be as careful or fear accidentally breaking them. Yet, I also preferred to be the one in charge. I had to take enough orders during my career as a soldier, and didn't want that same dynamic to follow me into the bedroom.

Unfortunately, large burly men who were also submissive were in short supply. It was one of the reasons I hadn't bothered to seriously pursue a relationship until now. One way or another, I always had to settle.

Ellis ticked all my boxes. Even the amnesia was a bit of a turn on, though I'd never admit such a thing out loud. He was a blank slate I could leave my mark on, and the sense of power that came with it was a heady sensation.

"Brody?" Ellis asked again when I didn't respond.

I'd been lost in my thoughts for too long. He was going to start thinking something was wrong.

Stepping back just enough to give him

some room, I cast the last of my doubt from my mind. Ellis didn't need uncertainty right now. He needed a steady hand.

"Get undressed."

He jumped and a smile broke out on his face as he immediately started undoing the buttons down his shirt. As I expected, he was much more comfortable with clear directions to follow.

His shirt hit the ground with a disproportionately loud sound. The only thing louder was the beating of my own heart pounding in my ears.

The dark curls on Ellis's head continued down over his chest as well. There was even an alluring trail over his stomach leading down to the waist of his pants. I ran a hand over his bare chest, then stroked up his neck until I was cupping his chin once again. Since he was sitting down, I had to lean forward to kiss him, but just before our lips touched,

I stopped.

"All of it."

"Huh?" Ellis said with a dazed voice.

We were so close my breath ghosted over his lips.

"Your clothes," I reminded him. "Take off all of them."

He swallowed a few times, swaying forward as if to chase the kiss that he anticipated.

I leaned back to avoid him. That wasn't how it worked. If he wanted something, he had to do as he was told first.

When our lips still didn't touch, Ellis jerked out of the daze he'd fallen into and finally registered what I was saying.

"What? Oh, right."

The last of his clothing was removed with the same lack of ceremony as his shirt. He sat on the bed, leaning back on his hands with his legs slightly parted so I could easily see all of him, completely unselfconscious.

It was a refreshing change to what I usually expected with partners. Those who were submissive were often shy as well. On the rare occasion when I found someone who wasn't shy, it usually came hand in hand with arrogance.

Ellis was none of those things. He was soft and eager to obey, but he was also very straightforward. Neither shy nor arrogant. He presented his body without any fanfare.

Maybe, without his memories, he had no reason to be self-conscious. There was nothing in his head telling him that nudity was something to be ashamed of.

Or maybe this was just how he was naturally. Either way, it was a win for me.

I pressed one knee against the edge of the bed, forcing him to spread his legs a little wider.

"Good boy." I carded my hand through his hair, and he leaned into my touch. "Such good behavior should be rewarded.

Is there anything that you want?"

It was only now that a blush of embarrassment spread over his cheeks. It was such an interesting contradiction. Nudity didn't affect him, but his own desires did.

Looking up at me through surprisingly long lashes, Ellis tugged at the button of my pants. "Can I?"

"Can you... what?" I had an idea of what he was asking for, but I wasn't going to make it easier for him. "Come on, Ellis. I need full sentences."

"Can I... use my mouth on you. I think that's something I enjoy. The idea feels right, at least."

Well, I'd never say no to that.

"Of course." My fingers remained tangled in his hair. "But you've got to do it yourself."

He nodded so quickly he nearly dislodged my hand, and immediately started undoing my pants. His back was to the window blocking the moonlight, so it took him a few times to get my fly open as his hands fumbled in the dark.

The moment my pants were open, and my arousal exposed to the air, there was no hesitation. He immediately wrapped his hands around my cock and his mouth descended upon me.

I gasped and clutched his shoulders for support against the sudden pleasure that shot through me like electricity. Until now, I'd been thinking of Ellis as a type of virgin, but that was wrong. The man clearly knew what he was doing as his lips and tongue pleasured me with expert skill. He somehow managed to find all my sensitive spots and even managed to swallow me to the back of his throat without any trouble.

And the man still didn't have his memories, meaning all of this came purely from muscle memory.

My view of Ellis shifted. The man acted

innocent, but once he regained his memory it was probably going to turn out that he had more experience than I did.

Not that I was complaining. Oh no. I certainly wasn't going to complain about his past sexual history when I was the one benefiting from it now.

It took an embarrassingly short amount of time before I was already approaching my end. Not wanting to finish so soon, I tugged on his hair to pull him away from me.

"Stop. Ellis, stop. Not yet."

He groaned, and the vibrations of his voice nearly sent me over the edge.

With one last harsh tug, I managed to dislodge him from me. He was panting and flushed, but there was a delighted gleam in his eyes.

"What?" he whined. "I wasn't done."

Pushing at his chest, I shoved him harshly back onto the bed and climbed over him.

"I'm not done, either. That's why you had to stop. There's more I want to do with you."

It was a stroke of luck that I kept the lube and condoms stored in my bedside table. Since I'd never brought a partner back to my house, and had no plans to do so, there was no reason to keep them close at hand. I'd only bought them on a hopeful whim and stored them in the nightstand because I had no other place for them.

I silently thanked my past self for the spontaneous decision as I grabbed the supplies from the drawer, grateful that I didn't have to leave the bed or even pull very far away from Ellis to reach them.

Unfortunately, that was where my luck ended. The lube bottle had never been used, and I had to fumble with the plastic seal around the cap to open it.

Ellis laughed. It was a breathless sound, but still obviously one of humor.

"Don't tell me you've never done this before. At least one of us needs to remember what they're doing."

"I have," I said through gritted teeth as I finally managed to get the damned bottle open. "Just not here."

"So, I'm the first in this bed."

He didn't say so, but I could tell that the thought made him happy from the way his eyes sparkled.

"Honestly, you're the first in a while. I've been too busy getting everything here built."

"Well..." He eyed me up and down, then relaxed back against the pillows and let his legs fall open wider, bracketing my hips on both sides. "I hope you still remember how it works."

That sounded like a challenge.

Coating my fingers in a generous amount of lube, I hitched one of his legs over my shoulder to open him up to me even more.

"See for yourself."

The first finger slid into him easily. He threw his head back, clinging to the headboard as a second finger quickly followed the first.

Yes. Ellis definitely had plenty of experience before. Even if his mind didn't remember, his body certainly did. There was a moment of resistance as internal muscles fought against the stretch of my fingers. But then, with a deep breath, Ellis relaxed, and I was able to press in even deeper.

"Fuuuck," Ellis groaned when I hit a particularly sweet spot inside him. "Y-you *do* know what you're doing."

"Told you."

I was already on edge, so I didn't bother prepping him for long. I needed to be inside him immediately, and from what I'd seen so far, his body would be able to take it.

He'd probably even like it a little

rough.

I rolled the condom on in record time, and a shiver traveled through me from head to toe when I finally slid inside him.

He was perfect. Just tight enough to feel good but without being difficult. His nails bit into my skin as he clung to my shoulders, and I couldn't help kissing him as I slowly pushed all the way inside. His moans mixed with my own. Each jerk of my hips brought a whole new slew of noises from both of us. If I weren't so pent up, I could have spent hours just experimenting with all the different sounds I could coax out of him.

Maybe another time. For now, I was too eager.

Almost as soon as I was all the way inside him, I immediately pulled out again. Ellis clung to me with both arms and legs, refusing to let me go. I pinned his arms down to the bed by his head, keeping him in place as I set the pace.

He whined and pleaded, begging me to fill him. The vulgar words coming from such a seemingly innocent mouth drove me crazy. I couldn't bear to wait for long. With one long, hard thrust, I drove all the way back inside his eager body.

His legs wrapped tight around me, and he sighed in relief.

I trailed my lips down from his mouth to his neck, where I'd already left several love bites. "Just as I thought. Someone likes it rough."

"Anything," Ellis babbled.

It wasn't clear if he even knew what he was saying, but I took him at his word. I started thrusting in earnest, setting a hard and fast pace that left us both gasping.

My fingers bit bruises into his wrists as I held him down. It was like he was made to take my cock, somehow always moving in just the right way to match me thrust for thrust and drive us both wild.

Pleasure tightened in my stomach and danced along my skin like electric fingers. I wasn't going to last.

Luckily, Ellis wasn't going to, either. We were both too pent up and it didn't take us long to reach the end of our patience.

It was like something exploded inside me. With one particularly hard thrust, lights bloomed behind my eyes like my own personal fireworks and ecstasy flooded through my veins. We came together, not so much falling over the edge of our orgasm as diving into it. A coppery taste spread across my tongue, making me tense up even more. In the height of passion, I'd bitten him, but he didn't seem to mind.

From the way he shuddered beneath me and painted both our stomachs with the evidence of his pleasure, he even seemed to like it.

We stayed locked together like that for

a while. My brain was full of static, like the constant back and forth rushing of the ocean. I could have easily fallen asleep right there, with little sparks of pleasure still making me twitch every now and then, but a voice in the back of my head said I needed to check on Ellis first.

"You okay?" I whispered against his neck. The bite mark I'd left on his skin wasn't too bad. I hadn't even broken the skin as much as I thought I had, though I reminded myself to spray the wound with disinfectant later, just in case.

At first, all Ellis could do was nod, but he eventually managed to squeeze out a few words.

"I'm... fine."

Taking a deep breath to shake a little more sense back into my brain, I shifted more of my weight onto my hands and knees. Ellis may have been a large man, but so was I, and it couldn't be comfortable being crushed under my weight.

Yet, I'd barely moved more than a few inches before Ellis's arms and legs were wrapping around me again, drawing me back to him.

"No," he groaned and hid his face against my chest. "Stay like this. Just a little longer."

It couldn't be comfortable. I was still buried inside him, and he barely had room to breathe, but I didn't argue. Instead, I merely tipped his chin up to face me.

"All right. I'll stay."

Then, as I resigned myself to the role of human blanket, I kissed him again.

***

It was nearly morning when I finally came to my senses. As the first rays of sun broke over the horizon, I sat on the edge of the bed staring out the window.

Ellis lay behind me, tangled in the bed

sheets and fast asleep.

"Fuck," I groaned as I ran a hand through my disheveled hair.

A headache was building behind my eyes, but I didn't bother to do anything about it.

I deserved the pain.

"I messed up."

I never should have gotten involved with Ellis. Maybe I shouldn't have even brought him home, but I never expected him to be such a successful temptation.

No. That made it sound like this was somehow his fault. The fault lay with me. I was the one who was weak. I was the one who had taken advantage of him. Sure, he'd consented and seemed to enjoy everything we did, but that didn't change the fact that he was completely reliant on me. The way things were now, nothing between us could ever be equal, but that hadn't stopped me from chasing my own desires last night.

I'd used him as a distraction. Even if he was a willing distraction, that didn't change the fact that I'd used him.

"Not again," I muttered to myself. "Never going to be that stupid again."

I groaned, slapped my cheeks a few times to wake myself up, and got out of bed. The sun was barely up, and I already felt like I needed a stiff drink.

Or ten.

I may be a degenerate, but I hadn't yet sunk so low that I would start getting drunk for breakfast.

Strong coffee would have to do.

Rounding the bed to approach my wardrobe, I noticed Ellis's clothes scattered over the floor. Ordinarily, I wouldn't touch a partner's clothes and let them handle their own laundry, but technically, they were my clothes so I didn't want them to get too wrinkled.

Picking the pieces up one by one, I tossed them into the hamper by the door to be cleaned and ironed later.

The last piece I picked up was the shirt. It was one of the few I owned that wasn't a plaid pattern of some sort, but it was still one of my favorites due to the deep pockets. I was very familiar with this shirt, so when I picked it up, I immediately realized something was wrong.

It was heavier than it should have been.

Weighing it in my hands for a moment, I soon traced the extra weight to a wooden box in the pocket.

I should have realized what I was holding the moment I laid eyes on the box, but my sleep and sex addled brain was particularly slow that morning. It wasn't until I opened the box and was staring down at its contents that the memories of yesterday came flooding back to me.

The key. In the chaos of finding out

about Creed's disappearance, I'd completely forgotten about Poppy Milford's key.

Slamming the box closed, I started pulling fresh clothes out of my wardrobe.

Magnus needed to know about this.

I could only hope he wasn't still mad at me.

CHAPTER SIX

Ellis

I WOKE UP to the noise of Brody hurriedly getting dressed.

"Wha...?"

I was almost as groggy as when I woke up for the first time in the hospital, and when I tried to sit up, I was sore.

Very sore.

After so long with an empty head, I wasn't used to being bombarded by memories upon waking. This time, moments after opening my eyes, images of the previous night flashed before my eyes.

Oh. So that's why I was sore.

Clearing my throat, I tried again. "Brody? What's going on?"

Brody froze with only one arm in his shirt and his pants hanging open on his hips.

"Ellis. Right... um..." It wasn't often that Brody lost his words, and the sight of him hesitating now made me nervous.

"Something's wrong." Sitting all the way up, I barely noticed that I was naked as I moved to the edge of the bed. "What happened? Did you hear something about Creed?"

There was an unrecognizable expression on Brody's face as he looked at me, almost like he was cringing in slow motion. I didn't know what it meant or what he was thinking, but it made something in the pit of my stomach drop.

With a sigh, Brody finished getting dressed, then sat next to me on the bed.

BRODY

"Nothing's happened. Well, at least nothing that hasn't already happened." He held up the wooden box with the key inside that we'd found buried in the woods. "I just need to tell Magnus about this. I forgot about it earlier, and he needs to know."

I breathed a sigh of relief. His distress had nothing to do with me. He and Magnus fought yesterday, so he must be worried about speaking with his friend. That was understandable.

"I'm sure Magnus isn't still upset. You two are friends, right. He'll talk to you."

I realized I was making a lot of assumptions about a situation I didn't understand. I barely knew Magnus, after all. Maybe the man was the type to hold a grudge after a single fight. Yet, I found that hard to believe. Brody considered Magnus a close friend, and anyone that Brody held in such high regard couldn't be a bad person.

Luckily, it seemed I was right, because Brody immediately nodded his head and agreed with me. "Yeah. You're right. Magnus burns hot, but he doesn't burn for long. He's probably already forgotten about last night."

There was that strange slow cringe expression again.

Was he lying and actually still worrying about Magnus, or was that expression caused by something else?

I got my answer a moment later.

"Look, Ellis..." Brody placed a hand on my leg that felt like it was supposed to be comforting, but the moment he made contact with my skin he pulled his hand away. "About last night... I'm sorry."

"Sorry?"

That didn't sound good. Nothing happy ever started with an apology. I didn't need my memories to know that much.

Brody couldn't look directly at me and occupied himself by buttoning up his shirt. "Yeah. It... it was a mistake. I never should have taken advantage of you like that."

"Advantage?" I tried to reach out to him, but he pulled away from me again, so I kept my hands to myself. "You didn't take advantage. I kissed you first. Remember? I definitely told you, multiple times, that I wanted it."

"Yeah," he agreed with me again, but his tone of voice still managed to make such a positive word sound like a death sentence. "But we have no way of knowing if you'd still agree if you had your memories. That feels like taking advantage."

"But I..." The words died on my tongue.

What could I even say?

I couldn't deny what he said. The truth was, I didn't know what the version of 'me' with memories would want. For all I knew, my non-amnesia self was a raging homophobe, and when I regained my memories, I would be horrified by what I'd done.

Still, that was my risk to take, and I was willing to take it. However, before I could argue, another thought occurred to me.

"You're right. We don't know who I really am. I might turn out to be a murderous thief on the run from the law. Not someone you'd want to get involved with."

I'd almost forgotten, but the vague memory of burying someone still lurked in my brain. Now, with the discovery of the key that had apparently been stolen from the police, my true identity wasn't looking very good.

Of course, Brody didn't want to risk getting in bed with a criminal.

Brody patted me on the shoulder, making sure to only touch me over the blanket that I had draped around me like a cloak.

"I really don't think you're some villainous murderer." For the first time since waking up, he looked directly in my eyes, and his gaze still held the comfort I'd become familiar with. "I've seen enough death, and enough hardened killers to know you're not one of them. There's a... callousness to life that is so deeply engrained in the real villains of the world that even amnesia wouldn't be able to get rid of. You don't have that. If you did bury someone, even if you killed them, you must have had a good reason. I'm certain about that."

A ray of morning sunlight snuck through the window, highlighting the dust hanging in the air around us and giving everything a natural halo. It would have been a perfect morning to wake up next to a love, free of all worries.

Instead, I was twisting the edge of the blanket between my hands as more and more unpleasant thoughts piled on top of me.

"I'll have to trust your opinion on it," I said, trying to add in a laugh and failing. "I certainly don't trust my own."

His gaze didn't stay on me as long as I would like. The moment I agreed with him, he looked away again.

"Good. So, um, I need to go talk to Magnus. Take your time getting dressed. My clothes are in the wardrobe there. Just take whatever you want for now. Hopefully, if there's time, we can take you to the store to get some of your own, but for now mine should do."

I kept looking down at my hands, even when he rose from the bed. Based on the sound of his footsteps, I tracked him as he moved around the room a bit more before leaving.

Then I was alone.

Even if I had my memories, I doubted I'd be able to describe what I was feeling.

Part of me was happy that Brody was so certain I couldn't have hurt anyone. It was a relief to know he thought so highly of me. If I had that same confidence in myself, nothing would ever bring me down again.

Yet, under that spark of joy, there was a tangled web of negative feelings. I enjoyed last night, and it hurt hearing Brody call it a mistake. He was right, of course. In the current situation, getting involved with anyone in such an intimate way was a bad idea.

My gaze turned to the wardrobe that Brody had given me free access to.

I had a roof over my head, clothes on my back, and three meals a day. None of which I was entitled to. Brody didn't have to give me anything, but he provided for all my needs without complaint. He'd even protected me when armed gunmen attacked us. Asking for anything more was just selfish.

I couldn't help wanting more, though. I'd been so happy last night. For the first time that I could remember, I felt like a real person and not just the shell of a person that my real self had left behind.

Was it really so bad to want more?

My stomach grumbled, interrupting my heavy train of thought. I snapped back to reality, and realized I couldn't hear Brody moving around anywhere in the house. There was no telling how long I'd been sitting there, but early morning was no time for deep self-reflection. I wasn't awake enough to handle the size of the questions bouncing around my head.

I got dressed quickly, grabbing whatever looked like it would fit me best. Most of Brody's clothes were the same "lumberjack chic" style. It looked good on him, but it didn't suit me. Instead, I managed to find a plain green shirt at the back of his closet, and a pair of dark jeans that mostly fit. He was a little taller than me, so I had to roll up the pants cuffs once to keep them from dragging on the ground, and his shoulders were a bit broader, so his shirt hung loosely on me, but otherwise it was close enough to be comfortable.

Plus, all his clothing smelled like him. When I pulled the shirt over my head, I pressed the collar to my nose for a moment, taking in the smell of cedar and bergamot. It was enough to chase the lingering tension from my shoulders and I left the bedroom with a thin shell of confidence.

As I suspected, Brody was no longer in the house. I found him outside, standing on the porch to Magnus's house. The door was open, and the two men faced each other across the threshold like it was a battleline.

Neither said a word for several moments, and I hung back on Brody's porch just a few yards away waiting to see what would happen.

"All right," Magnus eventually said, holding his arms out wide. "Let's get it over with."

At first, it looked like they were going to hug. I couldn't think of any other reason for a person to hold their arms out like that.

Then Brody cocked back his fist and punched Magnus hard in the shoulder.

"Fucking hell," Magnus shouted as he staggered and clutched his shoulder. "You really didn't hold back."

"That's what you get for being such a bastard."

"Yeah, yeah, yeah," Magnus muttered, though there was a smile on his face. "I was a jerk. I'm sorry. We good now?"

"We're good."

Trent came out of the house, fussing over Magnus's shoulder, but the blond man just waved off his concern. "All right. Now that that's over with, what was so urgent that you needed to talk to me this early in the morning." As he spoke, something seemed to occur to him, and he perked up. "Did you hear about Creed?"

"No," Brody shook his head. "It's something else. I forgot to tell you before, but look what we found yesterday."

He pulled out the wooden box and opened the lid. From this far away I couldn't see inside, but I could easily picture the key it held.

All three men stared down into the box for a moment, but surprisingly it was Trent that reached out and snatched up the key.

"This is Poppy Milford's key."

There was that name again. That was the same thing Brody had said when he saw the key, and it left me feeling like I was missing a big chunk of important information.

Magnus grabbed the key, not taking it

from Trent's hands, but turning it in the light to get a better view of its details.

"Are you sure?"

The look Trent gave him was so full of attitude that I could feel the heat from here. "Yes, I'm sure. I was called in to examine it for a reason. What? Do you doubt my judgment when it comes to an antique like this."

Magnus immediately let go of the key and backed away a few steps, practically hiding behind Brody. "No. No. Nope. Not doubting you at all. Don't listen to me. We've already established that I'm an idiot."

Brody snorted. "That's an understatement."

"Hey!" Magnus punched him in the shoulder, though it was clear he wasn't using anything close to his full strength. "Take that back."

The two of them were about to start bickering, when Trent interrupted.

"If we could focus, please. Brody, you said you found this yesterday?"

The playful air that surrounded them vanished, immediately turning serious once again. Even just sticking to basics, it took a while for Brody to explain everything that happened yesterday. He thankfully skipped over the part where I got confused between past and present and ran off into the woods thinking I was being chased, instead just saying that a few of my memories came back.

"But how did this key go from police custody to being buried in the woods a town over?" Magnus asked once Brody had finished his explanation. "Not to mention that it was apparently buried by the person you happened to hit with a tree. It's all just... really weird."

"We don't really know how the key and the journal went missing," Trent pointed out, still turning the key over in his hands and holding it up close to his eye like he thought he might find an explanation inscribed in the metal. "Deputy Hillard just said that the key and the journal were stolen, but didn't really explain how it happened. That might be a good place to start."

With a heavy sigh, Brody pulled out his phone. "I'll give him a call. Maybe we can convince him to tell us more."

Apparently, calling this Deputy Hillard person was easier said than done. Brody spent half an hour on the phone, making various calls until he finally managed to speak with the man in question, and then another twenty minutes locked in a heated argument. He stepped away from all of us during this time, so I couldn't hear what was being said, but I could tell it was an argument just from the way he kept moving his arms when he talked.

While waiting for Brody to get off the phone, Trent threw together a simple breakfast, which he passed around to everyone, including me. I was still sitting on the front porch, watching Brody from a distance, and didn't hear Trent approach, so I was startled when a plate of toast and eggs was suddenly shoved under my nose.

"Oh, um. Thanks." I took the plate and picked up a piece of toast.

"It'll be okay," Trent said as he sat beside me, balancing his own plate in one hand.

"Why do people keep trying to comfort me?" I asked as I poked at the eggs with my fork. "Do I really look that upset?"

"No." Trent took a bite of his own eggs and chewed for a moment as he thought. "But you do look... I guess *lost* would be the best word. Your gaze hasn't left Brody for more than a few seconds since coming out here. Plus, well..." He awkwardly cleared his throat then tapped the side of his neck. "There's also... that."

I had no idea what he was talking

about, and only got more confused as he continued to tap the side of his neck with emphasis. My hand instinctively came up to my own neck, and I flinched when I felt the raised skin there.

A memory of Brody biting me the night before played out in my mind, and I had to bite my own lip to keep from making any embarrassing sounds.

"I have to ask," Trent said after a moment when I remained silent. "It was... consensual, right?"

"Yes!"

I didn't mean to shout, but the word came tumbling out of me so quickly I couldn't control it. All three dogs lazing around the property jumped to their feet, and even Brody and Magnus looked over at us. Trent quickly waved them away and they went back to what they were doing.

My face burned with mortification, and I shoved a few bites of breakfast into my mouth just to give myself something to do. Unfortunately, I forgot what was on my plate, and flinched when the taste of eggs hit my tongue.

It turned out my previous assumption was true. I really hated eggs. The texture was unpleasant, and the taste made me gag, but I forced myself to swallow, so I didn't insult Trent.

He probably knew anyway, based on the way I immediately downed half the glass of orange juice that had also been provided, but he was nice enough not to comment on my reaction.

"Yes," I tried again once I'd cleared the taste of eggs from my mouth. "It was consensual. I promise."

Trent nodded, clearly not surprised by my statement. "I figured as much, but I just had to check."

He stood up like he was about to leave, probably to go back to Magnus, but I stopped him.

"Um, Trent?" My voice sounded so

small, I tugged on his sleeve just to make sure he heard me. "I appreciate your concern but, would you have asked me that if I didn't have amnesia?"

Surprised flashed across his face for a moment, but it disappeared as quickly as it came and he sat back down next to me, closer than before.

"Honestly, probably not. But your situation is unique so we can't be too careful."

With a slow nod, I stuffed the last piece of toast into my mouth, then set the eggs aside so I didn't accidentally eat any more. The toast was dry and took a minute of chewing and the rest of my orange juice to get down, which gave me enough time to process what he'd said.

"So, it's true," I eventually concluded once I was able to talk again. "Without memories, I really can't consent, even if I wanted to."

"Hey…" Trent set his own plate aside.

"That's not what I said. I just wanted to double check."

"No, but it's what Brody said. He thinks he took advantage of me and that last night was a mistake. He's probably right. Not about taking advantage, but about the mistake."

The dogs came sniffing around our plates, looking for scraps. Trent reached around me and dumped the eggs I clearly didn't want on the ground from them to eat.

At least the food wasn't wasted.

"Do you think it was a mistake?" Trent asked as he stored my now empty plate under his own.

"No, but... I'm not really a person, so I can't make that decision."

I could feel Trent's scowl even without looking at him. "Don't say that. You are a person."

"No, I'm not. I'm just an empty shell, like the remains left on the beach after a crab molts. It may have the same shape as the crab, and a person looking at it might even mistake it for a crab, but there's nothing inside."

Trent grabbed my arm, cutting off my rant that was building up.

"That's not true. A person is more than just their memories, and I'm sure Brody doesn't see you as an empty shell."

"Well, he certainly doesn't think I'm someone worth getting involved with. I'm just a mistake. He made that clear this morning."

The venom in my voice surprised even myself. I thought I'd accepted Brody's decision, but apparently it bothered me more than a realized. Acid churned in my stomach, and for a moment I feared I would bring up what little breakfast I'd managed to eat.

Trent just rubbed my shoulders for a moment as I got myself under control.

"You know," he eventually spoke up.

"Just because Brody thinks sleeping with you was a mistake, doesn't mean he thinks *you* are a mistake. Brody and Magnus are both good guys, and good guys like them would much rather walk away than risk causing unnecessary harm."

"Soooo," I drew out that one word, giving myself a moment to think. "You're saying I should keep going after him?"

Trent just shrugged but there was a smile on his face. "Hey, you're a person who can make his own decisions. I can't tell you what to do."

From there, the rest of our conversation was much lighter, but Trent's suggestion continued to circulate in the back of my mind. A few minutes later, Brody finished his phone call and returned, announcing that he would be going into town to meet with Deputy Hillard in person so they could discuss things face to face.

"Magnus and I will stay here," Trent spoke up before anyone else could say a word. "While you're doing that, we'll see if we can find out anything more about what happened to Creed."

This idea was immediately accepted, and with the decision made, everyone went their separate ways. Brody headed for his truck, while Trent and Magnus returned to Magnus's house to continue the search for Creed.

Just before he shut the door, Trent gave me a pointed look and nodded in Brody's direction.

I hesitated for a moment, but just before Brody reached his truck, I managed to find my courage.

"Brody, wait up." I ran off the porch. "I'm coming with you."

CHAPTER SEVEN

Brody

"NO."

My voice wasn't as strong as I wanted, but even that single word was enough to put a frown on Ellis's face.

"Give me one good reason why I can't come inside with you."

I sighed and pinched the bridge of my nose. There was nothing I could say that I hadn't said a dozen times already, but I tried anyway.

"Because this meeting doesn't concern

you and there's no reason to put yourself in the middle of it."

I shouldn't have let him come. He'd somehow got his hands on Poppy Milford's key and buried it in the woods, so it was clear he was involved in everything that was happening. However, without his memories, there was no way to know his initial intentions. Plus, even if Ellis was just an innocent bystander who'd been dragged into this, he already had enough problems on his plate. He should just remain somewhere safe and focus on getting his memories back.

For all these reasons, I didn't want him to come along with me when I went to visit Deputy Hillard.

Unfortunately, he'd climbed into my truck before I could object and refused to get out no matter how I tried to argue. Ellis wasn't a fighter, but he was also a large man, and forcibly pulling him out of the truck without hurting him would be a struggle.

Magnus had turned out to be no help, either. He and Trent had just watched with amused looks on their faces from the porch of Magnus's house as I ordered, argued, and pleaded with Ellis to get out of the truck.

It was no use. In the end, I had to bring Ellis along with me or I'd end up completely missing my meeting with Deputy Hillard.

The ride into town had been uncomfortably silent. It was clear Ellis had something to say, but the few times he turned to me and opened his mouth like he was about to speak, no words came out and he eventually, went back to watching the trees pass by the window.

Thankfully, the drive into town didn't take too long.

Emberwood was a very small town with only one main road. Most buildings didn't even have proper addresses and were merely differentiated by whether they were on the north side or the south side of the main road. The town's small police station was on the north side, but I kept driving until I pulled up to a little diner on the south side. It was a small building, only big enough to fit about a dozen tables. From the outside, it didn't look like a diner. The building had once been a carriage house, and when the new owners bought it to turn it into a restaurant, they couldn't bear to alter the hand-carved woodwork that decorated the outside.

So, they'd left everything the same and simply painted the door a bright shade of blue to make it stand out. The restaurant didn't even have a name. Everyone simple referred to it as "The Blue Door."

Pulling into one of the limited parking spots on the street outside the diner, I turned the ignition off.

The silence stretching between us

didn't last for long as Ellis was eager to continue our argument.

"You can't say this has nothing to do with me. I may not remember what happened, but it's clear that I was involved somehow. Between the key I buried in the woods, and the *Mothers of the Mountain*, and the body you found, something is clearly going on that I'm involved with. I can't just sit back and… and do nothing."

I shouldn't get mad at him. It was no surprise that he was being stubborn about this.

Hell, if I was in his shoes, I'd probably be twice as stubborn. But I couldn't help it. The thought of dragging him into danger filled me with a sense of dread I couldn't explain.

I gripped the steering wheel so hard my knuckles turned white. Taking a deep breath, I forced myself to relax and pried my hands off the wheel.

"Ellis, I'm going in there to meet with Deputy Hillard, and you are going to sit here and stay out of the way. I don't need you to interfere. You're already more involved than you should be, so for now, you just need to stay out of the way. Understood?"

Although Ellis was a large man, he still managed to slump down in his seat so far that he almost looked like a chastised child.

"Yeah. Got it. You don't need me. You've made that... you've made that very clear."

I'd been through a lot of shit in my life, some of it my own doing, but I'd never felt worse than I did in that moment as I walked away from the truck. I kept an ear tuned to the sound of the door opening to make sure Ellis didn't follow me, but I couldn't bear to look back and see him sitting there with that defeated expression on his face.

BRODY

A decent person would have gone back. A decent person would apologize and find some way to work things out, rather than just walk away.

I kept walking and stepped through the door of the diner.

It was just another example of why we shouldn't get involved with each other. I wasn't a decent enough person.

There weren't many customers in the diner, but due to its small size, most of the tables were still full. I could see everything from the front door, so it wasn't hard to spot Deputy Hillard sitting in the far back corner. We locked eyes for a moment, but he didn't make any other move to draw attention to my presence.

"We could have met at your office," I said as I pulled out a chair at his table. "Assuming that rundown little station of yours even has offices."

Deputy Hillard prodded with his fork at the barely touched plate of pancakes sitting in front of him.

"We do, but it's not... it's just good to get out of the office when I can."

Translation: he feared being overheard by his own coworkers.

This meant that either his investigation into the body found on our property and the stolen items was being done "off the books", or he suspected that one of his own coworkers was involved.

That explained the barely touched meal in front of him. Coming to a diner without ordering anything would look suspicious, but there weren't many places in this small town where two people could meet up without drawing attention.

The waitress came by, and I ordered a basic cup of coffee, but waved away the menu. I had no intention of hanging around long enough for a pretend meal.

"All right," I said once the waitress had left. "No more stalling. I've already told you everything I know on the phone. Now, it's time for you to start talking."

I could see the hesitation that still lingered in Deputy Hillard's eyes, but it wasn't as strong as it once was. After everything that had happened to us— being robbed and spied on, Magnus and Trent being drugged, and now Ellis and me openly attacked at gunpoint—even Deputy Hillard had to admit that we deserved to know the truth.

Sighing heavily, the other man pushed away the cold plate of pancakes. "Were do I even start?"

"How about the beginning?"

"The beginning?" He laughed under his breath with a slow, sad sound. "The beginning starts over a century ago."

"Why am I not surprised?"

The waitress chose that moment to return with my coffee, and we both waited in awkward silence until she left.

Staring down into the dark liquid in my cup, I was reminded of another mystery that I'd forgotten about. The coffee beans we'd found inside Rose Milford's locket were still unexplained.

I stared at Deputy Hillard over the rim of my mug as I took a sip. We'd switched out the coffee beans when we gave him the locket.

Did he know?

Would he try to trick me the same way we'd tricked him?

I had no reason to trust what he said, but I also had no other place to look for information.

It wasn't a great position to be in, but I didn't let any of that show on my face as I held his gaze.

"I'm not going to sit around here all day. If this all started a hundred and twenty-five years ago, then you've got a long story to tell. So, start talking."

Each second felt like an hour as I waited for him to find his words. Finally, after a lifetime of patience—which was probably only about thirty seconds—he spoke up.

"You know about how the Milford sisters came to this town, right? They just wandered out of the woods one day without an explanation. From what I've been told, they were barely more than teenagers at the time. Early twenties, at most, but there was something about them that made them seem much older. They got jobs at the town's mill and lived quietly until people started to notice something strange about them. Their garden was ten times more fruitful than anywhere else, and they gave away their surplus of food. They healed illnesses, could fix anything that was broken, and could even tell the future. They predicted the fire that destroyed the town, saving most of the people. The few people who did die in the fire were corrupt individuals that everyone wanted to get rid of. After that, the head of the Milford family took over as mayor, adopted the sisters as his daughters, and the town was renamed Emberwood."

"Then a cult was formed around these newly crowned *'Mothers of the Mountain'* and everyone lived happily ever after," I said with as much sarcasm as I could muster before taking another sip of coffee. "I've heard your fairytale before, but none of that explains what's happening now."

Deputy Hillard quickly waved his hand in front of me, silently begging me to lower my voice as he looked around nervously. "I'm getting to that. I just wanted to make sure we were on the same page, and explain why, even now, the reverence for the three sisters is still so strong. There are a lot of people in this town who wouldn't be alive today if their families weren't saved from that fire all those years ago. And it's not just the fire. Drought. Famine. Plague. War. None of it was able to touch Emberwood while the

Mothers of the Mountain were here, and even now, the town is relatively prosperous despite its small size."

I'd never agreed with religious worship of any kind. It all felt very silly and impractical to me. If you wanted something to happen, you had to achieve it with your own hands. Praying to a god to solve your problems for you was not only a waste of breath, but also a lazy way to avoid putting in real work.

Although, I supposed it was better that the ancestors of this town at least worshiped something that was tangible. If the sisters were able to accomplish even half of what the stories said about them, it was no wonder other people ended up worshiping them.

"Okay. I get it. These sisters are really important to a lot of people. I'll try not to rock too many boats, but if people keep attacking me and my friends, then I can't guarantee anything."

"I know," Deputy Hillard nodded, swirling the last dregs of his own cup of coffee. "It never should have gotten this far, but that body you found has stirred up a lot of hostilities." He sighed again, and I nearly reached over the table to grab him and shake the answers out of him.

I didn't need a long-winded story about the town's history. I just needed to know how to keep my own people safe.

"The story of the *Mothers of the Mountain* has been told over and over," Deputy Hillard finally said, though it sounded like every word had to be forcibly dragged out of him. "But there's one part of the story that is always glossed over. The sisters' initial arrival in town. They just walked out of the woods one day, with no indication where they came from."

I couldn't contain the snort that escaped from my nose, and quickly took another sip of coffee to try and hide my reaction. "I'm sure your cult has come up with all kinds of supernatural explanations. They were born to a pack of wolves? Or maybe they were actually fallen stars that took human form." I snapped my fingers as a new idea came to me. "Oh. I know. They grew up out of the ground and bloomed from flowers. It would explain their names."

Based on the way his expression shifted, I could tell I'd hit the nail on the head with my last guess. Deputy Hillard cleared his throat and waved down the waitress for a refill on his drink, never once meeting my eye.

"Something like that used to be the common belief," he mumbled once the waitress left. The diner wasn't very loud since it could only hold a handful of customers, but I could still barely hear him over the chatter of the couple at the table next to us.

I leaned back in my chair, conscious of

the creak of old wood. These chairs had not been made for someone of my size and weren't very comfortable. Every time I moved, I feared it would collapse under me, but I still tried to look as relaxed as possible.

"Cults are all the same. Always trying to make their story seem more extraordinary than it really is."

"It's not like that," Deputy Hillard snapped, clearly bothered by my repeated use of the word "cult".

I just smirked at him, gloating at the fact that I'd gotten under his skin.

Realizing he'd reacted exactly as I wanted, he tried to rein himself back in. "I mean... obviously we know that those stories were just a work of fiction. The *Mothers of the Mountain* are humans like everyone else. And as humans, they had to come from somewhere. That's what this all boils down to. Where the three sisters came from before they appeared in

Emberwood."

"And where is that?" I demanded, already getting fed up. "You're really beating around the bush. After all the buildup you're giving to this information, it had better be something fantastic."

I could have been home right now helping Magnus hunt down information about Creed. Or even with Ellis doing… nothing. We would be doing nothing at all together because I'd already decided that getting involved with him was a bad idea.

Even the one night we'd spent together was already going too far.

My gaze instinctively shifted toward the window. The shades were mostly drawn, so I could only see the tail end of my truck. He was still sitting in there, waiting for me.

Hopefully. After the way our conversation had ended, I wouldn't be surprised if he chose to disappear off into the woods like he'd tried to do before.

A bubble of hysterical laughter welled up in my stomach as I realized Ellis had come into my life in the same way that the Milford sisters had wandered into town.

Well, almost the same. I doubted the sisters ever had a tree dropped on them.

Maybe that was the key to Ellis's identity. The sisters actually were witches, and Ellis was the reincarnation of one of them.

On the other side of the table, Deputy Hillard never noticed my distraction. He was too lost in his own thoughts as he recounted a story that he cared about a lot more than I did.

"Their origins weren't discovered until years after the *Mothers of the Mountain* settled in Emberwood. Before coming here, the sisters were part of a cult on the other side of the mountain. *The Tamed Souls.* They are a small but fanatical group that are focused on 'returning to a time of order and innocence by living simply away from the chaos of modern society'. That's literally a word for word description I've seen on their recruiting material."

A car alarm started going off outside, disrupting the otherwise peaceful atmosphere of the morning. A few of the diner's customers grumbled, but no one paid the noise much attention.

I barely even noticed as I scoffed at Deputy Hillard. "Ha. They left one cult to create their own. Why am I not surprised?"

"Oh, no," Deputy Hillard quickly corrected me. "*The Mothers of the Mountain* were not willing members of *The Tamed Souls*. They were born to it and weren't allowed to leave. They eventually managed to escape and hid in the forest, traveling on foot all the way to the other side of the mountain until they eventually ended up here."

I wanted to scoff again, but I couldn't bring myself to do it. During my time in the service, I'd encountered several cults and other fanatical groups. The young women raised in these kinds of environments were rarely treated well. It was no surprise that the Milford sisters had run away, and deep down, I was impressed by the fact that they'd managed to successfully escape.

If their actions in the past weren't interfering with my own life so much right now, I might have even admired them.

The car alarm outside was still blaring.

Why wasn't the owner shutting it off?

"I'm still failing to see why any of this affects us now."

"Because..." Deputy Hillard looked around the diner before leaning closer to me and whispering. "*The Tamed Souls* are still around, and they claim that the *Mothers of the Mountain* stole something from their leader when they escaped. No one knows what it is, but *The Tamed Souls* really want it back."

"*The Tamed Souls*," I repeated, staring blankly at him. "So, you're saying this other cult is behind everything that's happening?"

"Yes. We aren't sure how, or even when, they found out about the *Mothers of the Mountain*, but ever since then they've targeted us. They'd been silent for a while, until you uncovered that coffin."

Closing my eyes, I took a deep breath as a feeling of resignation settled over me.

"The locket, the key, and the journal that we found. These wouldn't happen to be what the sisters stole from *The Tamed Souls*, would it?"

The answer would make sense, but Deputy Milford immediately shook his head.

"No. I don't know what was stolen but based on the reaction I've seen from people who are part of *The Tamed Souls*, these items aren't what they are looking for. However, they do think that these items might lead to whatever they are looking for, which is why they stole the key and the journal. They've even tried to steal the locket, though we've managed to keep that one safe, at least."

That explained who stole the key and the journal, and also why Ellis and I were attacked.

But how had Ellis ended up with the key in the first place?

Was he a member of *The Tamed Souls*?

No. That didn't make sense.

If he was a member of *The Tamed Souls* then why would he hide the key from them, and why would he have been running from them in the first place?

A crucial piece of information was still missing, locked away in Ellis's missing memories.

Before I could demand any more answers, I was interrupted by one of the other customers unexpectedly shouting.

"Oh my god! Look! Someone's truck is being stolen!"

Several people clustered around the diner's windows, pressing their noses to the glass for a better view of whatever action was happening outside. Curiosity got the better of me, and I looked over as well.

Only to see the tail end of my own truck, with the rear lights flashing in time to the wailing alarm.

I jumped up, shouting as I knocked over my chair and raced for the door. The diner was small, yet it felt like it spanned miles as I pushed people aside to get to my truck. I felt like an idiot for not recognizing the sound of my own emergency alarm. I'd bought the truck just before moving here, so I hadn't had it long enough to hear the alarm very often, but some instinct still should have alerted me that something was wrong.

My irritation at Deputy Hillard must have distracted me. I was such an idiot. I should have known better than to let my guard down and not take the situation seriously. When I was on active duty, this kind of oversight would have gotten me killed.

Now, it might be someone else's life that paid the price.

When I finally pushed my way outside, I stumbled right into a nightmare. Several armed men surrounded my truck, and the passenger side door was open. Right before my eyes, Ellis was pulled out of the truck, kicking and screaming all the way. He put up a decent fight, until one good punch to the face dropped him to the ground.

I saw red.

It was just like being back on the battlefield. My instincts were still nearly as sharp as they had been, and barely a heartbeat passed before I smashed my fist into the nearest assailant's face. My body moved without thought, and in that moment, I felt like I was twenty years old again. Before the first assailant had even hit the ground, I was already grabbing the gun out of their hand.

It was just a handgun, so it lacked the precision and power that I usually preferred from my weapons. But it would do.

Standing in the middle of the sidewalk, I aimed and put two bullets into the next assailant. There wasn't even time for them to turn around, so I ended up shooting them directly in the back. It wasn't an honorable kill, but it was effective.

Behind me, I could hear the faint sound of screaming. People inside the diner were panicking, as what they thought was simply a carjacking turned into a lethal shootout.

That was fine. So long as they didn't get in my way, they could scream all they liked.

I managed to kill one more of the assailants before the rest of them noticed what was happening and started firing back, forcing me to take cover behind my truck. As bullets ricocheted off the truck's frame, I was glad that I'd decided to go with such a sturdy model. This was the truck's second gunfight in just a few days, and it was holding up surprisingly well.

There were too many bullets flying for me to make my way around the front of the truck, but luckily, I'd left the windows down for Ellis when I went inside the diner. I refused to think about how the lowered windows were probably how the assailants got Ellis out of the tuck in the first place and focused only on the opportunity it provided me.

Aiming my gun through the open windows, I managed to get one assailant in the leg, and clip another's shoulder.

They would survive, but the injuries

were severe enough that they weren't able to continue to participate in the fight. I should have been happy about that. Ending a conflict with minimal casualties should have been a good thing, but all I could feel was disappointment.

I wanted them dead. I wanted everyone who dared to hurt the people I cared about—hurt Ellis—to bleed out on the concrete.

Just as I was trying to figure out my next move, the gunfire suddenly stopped. Dread washed over me. There was no good reason for the assailants to let up their assault when they still had the upper hand.

Keeping my finger on the trigger of my gun, I peered around the front of my truck.

There were only three assailants left in fighting condition. Less than I originally thought. Two of them stood with their guns firmly pointed in my direction, flanking the last assailant who was clearly the leader. All of them wore masks over their faces, so I couldn't see them, but that didn't stop me from glaring directly into their eyes when I saw what had caused them to stop shooting.

The leader's gun wasn't pointed at me. Instead, they had one arm wrapped around Ellis's throat, and their gun pointed directly at his head.

Ellis groaned and tugged at the arm around his throat, but he was still dazed from the blow he'd taken earlier. He may as well have tried to fend them off with a feather for all the effect his struggling had. Blood dripped down his face from a gash on his forehead and matted the thick hair on the side of his head.

I clenched my gun so hard it shook, but I didn't press the trigger. As much as I wanted to kill them, I couldn't take the risk.

The assistants said nothing. They

made no threats or demands. They simply kept the gun pointed at Ellis's head as they dragged him toward the back of a waiting van.

I'd been wrong. When Ellis and I were attacked before, I'd assumed that they were after me and that Ellis's involvement was just collateral damage.

Now it was clear that Ellis had been their target all along.

I spat every curse I could think of under my breath as I watched Ellis disappear inside the van.

Still, I waited.

The moment for action came when the final assailant jumped inside the van. It was only a split second, but in order to climb inside the van they had to stop aiming their gun.

My finger squeezed the trigger faster than my brain could think. It was muscle memory at this point to shoot the moment an opportunity arose. There was no hesitation. No second-guessing. Just a familiar popping sound, a jolt against my wrist as I fought to keep the gun steady, and then my target was clutching a freshly bleeding wound.

Damn. I'd missed. As I'd feared, the handgun wasn't as accurate as I'd like, and I'd only grazed my target.

The last assailant stumbled into the van and the doors slammed closed just as the engine revved. They were about to escape. About to get away from me.

No.

I wouldn't allow it.

Tossing the disappointing handgun aside, I grabbed the rifle I had strapped to the rack in the back of my truck, then jumped behind the wheel. I lost precious seconds fumbling with the keys to get my truck started, and by the time I put it in drive, the van with Ellis inside was already careening down the street.

My foot was already on the gas when

my passenger door swung open. Deputy Hillard was nearly knocked off his feet as he dove inside my already moving truck.

"Drive," he ordered as he struggled to right himself in the seat and close the door behind him.

"I don't need your order," I said through gritted teeth as I steered my truck onto the street, pushing it as fast as it would go.

"Actually, you do." Deputy Hillard held up his badge. "Have you forgotten that you're a civilian now. You're subject to the laws just like everyone else, and driving hell bent down the road in a dangerous high-speed chase is illegal. But now you can technically say that this chase was sanctioned by a member of law enforcement."

We were gaining on the van. On an open road, the van might have had the upper hand, but on the twisting roads of a small mountain town, even a racecar could only go so fast.

"Fine," I said, pressing my truck's accelerator all the way down to the floor. "If you're going to be here, then make yourself useful and figure out a way to stop that van."

After considering it for a moment, Deputy Hillard pulled his revolver from the holster at his hip and leaned out the window to aim at the van. He fired a few times, each shot hitting the back of the van, but it made no difference. The bullets had no more effect than pebbles.

One of the assailants leaned out the van window and returned fire. The bullet took out my side mirror, and Deputy Hillard barely managed to duck back inside the truck to avoid the shot.

"Fuck. I think the van is armored. Taking it out won't be so easy."

I scoffed and wanted to roll my eyes, but I didn't dare look away from the van. We'd completely left the main roads behind and were quickly approaching the edge of town.

"Useless." Still keeping one hand on the wheel, I reached for the rifle I'd grabbed earlier. "Let me take care of it. Just grab the wheel."

"What?"

I don't bother to explain as I abandoned the wheel to hang the upper half of my body out the window. Deputy Hillard shouted and grabbed the wheel as the truck swerved, but he managed to keep it under control.

"Are you crazy?"

"Hmmm..." I thought it over for a second as I lined my eye up to the scope of my gun. "Probably."

I fired, and the rifle made an impressive sound as it kicked back harshly into my shoulder.

The bullet put a sizable hole in the back of the van's bumper.

"Holy shit!" Deputy Hillard cursed and

his grip on the wheel wavered for a moment causing us to swerve. "What kind of modifications do you have on that thing? Do you have a license for that?"

It was only thanks to my use of experience that I managed to keep my gun steady as Deputy Hillard struggled to get the truck back under control.

"Yep. I'd show you my license, but I'm a little busy right now."

The moment the truck straightened out, I fired again, blowing out one of the van's back wheels.

The whole vehicle jerked, but it should have been able to keep going. A deflated wheel shouldn't have been enough to stop such a sturdy vehicle, but luck wasn't on their side. The tire blew at exactly the same moment as they hit a large root that was growing across the road. The combined effect was enough to make the van swerve out of control. They fishtailed, tires struggling to find traction on the dirt road, and their back end knocked against a tree. Vans were naturally more top heavy, and at such a high speed, the impact caused the whole van to flip.

I hit the brakes to keep from crashing into them and was helpless to do anything but watch as the van rolled over several times. There was a chilling shriek of bending metal as with each roll the van made it twist more and more out of shape.

I forgot to even put my truck in park as I jumped out the door and ran for the van.

"Ellis!"

One of the van's doors fell off its hinges and a body fell out.

It wasn't Ellis. Even without seeing their face, I knew just from their physique that it was one of the assailants.

And they were still alive. They groaned as they crawled away from the wreckage, injured but clearly alive.

Deputy Hillard ran past me and

grabbed the assailant's arm. "You're under arrest. Anything you say—"

He never got to finish reciting the Miranda Rights as I raised my rifle and shot the assailant directly in the head.

Deputy Hillard jumped back. "What the hell? You can't just..."

He trailed off as I stepped over the fresh body, kicking it over with my foot as I went. My modified rifle was no joke, and the entire back of the assailant's head was now gone.

"Yes, I can." I paused when I reached Deputy Hillard. "Are you going to stop me?"

Deputy Hillard quickly shook his head. He was more afraid of me in that moment than he had been during the entire car chase and gunfight.

Good. That would make things easier.

I approached the back of the van with my gun reloaded and at the ready. This one was going to haunt me. Right now, adrenaline was surging through my veins, so I wasn't feeling anything but righteous fury, but once I calmed down, I knew the memory of the lives I took today would keep me awake at night for a while. I'd made it a point to make sure that killing never became easy. I didn't want to be one of those people who held such little regard for life.

But that didn't mean I wouldn't fight. When the situation called for it, I would still pull the trigger without hesitation.

I would just suffer for it later.

Some luck was on my side. The crash had killed the other assailants for me. They must have been standing in the back of the van when the crash happened and bounced around inside it like pinballs when the van flipped. Both of their necks were broken, and they lay in crumpled heaps among the wreckage.

"Ellis?" I called as I searched the bodies for any sign of the man. "Ellis?

Answer me, damn it."

I eventually found him hanging upside-down from the ceiling. He was strapped into a chair that had once been bolted to the side of the van, but with the van lying on its side, he was now dangling from the ceiling.

My fingers pressed against his neck.

His pulse hammered under my touch. He was alive.

Gasping with a sigh of relief, I rushed to find a way to get him down. "Hold on, Ellis. I've got you. Just... hold on."

He didn't make a sound. Even when I finally managed to free him from the straps keeping him in place, he didn't so much as twitch.

I carefully carried Ellis out of the van and laid him on the ground.

He looked worse in the sunlight. The blood staining his skin was bright red, drawing attention to how pale his olive complexion had become.

"I've called an ambulance," Deputy Hillard said as he also knelt beside Ellis. "Is he all right?"

"I don't know." I tapped Ellis's cheek a couple of times, trying to get some sort of reaction from him. "Ellis. Come on. Give me something."

He stayed as silent as the dead. While he may have been alive, nothing I did would wake him up.

CHAPTER EIGHT

HE DOESN'T WANT me.

This thought kept bouncing around my head. I wasn't surprised when he said he didn't need me. That I already knew. Brody was a self-sufficient man who seemed to have everything in his life figured out and could handle anything that came his way.

I, on the other hand, was an amnesiac mess that may or may not be a criminal and needed other people to make my decisions for me.

No, Brody definitely didn't need me, but I'd been hoping he at least wanted me.

After the conversation we'd just had, that wasn't looking like a possibility, either. The man might like me physically, our one night together made that clear, but he didn't want me around more than necessary.

As I sat in Brody's parked truck feeling like a fool, I contemplated my options. The windows were down and a pleasant breeze blew across my face, in stark contrast to my very unpleasant thoughts.

Without my memories, I couldn't leave Brody, but what if they never came back. He wasn't going to support me forever.

Where would I even go?

I still had no idea who I even was, and so far, there hadn't been much luck identifying me. When I was in the hospital the police had taken my blood to try a

DNA match, but that had turned up nothing. No relatives or friends had shown up looking for me, and there was no missing person's report matching my description.

Maybe I should just live in the woods, taking shelter in a tent and hunting my own food. I could do odd jobs under the table for some cash and live completely off the grid.

At least that way I wouldn't bother anyone.

I never saw the hand reaching for me until it gripped over my mouth and pressed my head back against the truck's seat. I tasted leather as I tried to scream, but nothing more than a muffled noise came out. Someone was leaning through the window, masked and gloved so barely any of their skin was showing.

"Shut up," the person hissed at me. A male voice.

"Don't bother," another person said

behind the one silencing me. "Just bring him."

With my head pinned, I couldn't see the second speaker, and their voice was more androgynous so I couldn't even tell if they were male or female.

My breath came in harsh little bursts through my nose as panic made my vision go blurry around the edges. "Bring him" could only be interpreted one way. I was being abducted and based on the number of voices I heard contemplating how to get me out of the truck, there were multiple people involved.

I probably couldn't even fight off one. A whole group would be impossible.

Brody could fight off a group. I'd seen him do it before.

The man holding my face pressed my back harder into the seat to keep me in place as he reached for the unlock button on the door. My seatbelt wasn't on. If they got the door open, they could easily pull me out, and then it would all be over.

Luckily, my arms were still free.

Before the man could reach the unlock button, I knocked his hand away just enough to pull the door handle. With the door still locked, pulling the handle from the inside set off the alarm.

The man holding me jerked back in surprise as the alarm wailed, and I got a good look at all my attackers for the first time. It was worse than I feared. Not only was there a whole group of people surrounding the truck, but they were heavily armed as well.

Even if I tried escaping through a different door, a different kidnapper would just grab me. They had me thoroughly surrounded.

The alarm didn't distract them for long. Another person reached around the first man and unlocked the door, allowing them to open it and grab me by the front of my shirt.

I braced my hands and feet against the inner wall of the truck, wedging myself inside as best as possible.

"You fucker," one of the kidnappers gasped as they struggled to pull me from the truck.

For once, I was glad for my size. It made it harder for them to move me against my will.

I kicked out blindly and managed to hit one of them hard enough to knock them away, but another body just took their place. It was a losing battle. I couldn't fight them off, but maybe I could buy enough time for Brody to notice what was happening.

Once again, I had no choice but to rely on him to save me. I really was completely useless.

It ended when one of the kidnappers got fed up with the struggle and punched me in the stomach. The sudden pain made me curl up, and they were able to drag me from the truck. I still tried to fight back, flailing like a drunken madman with no fighting skills, but another punch to the face made my whole world spin and I dropped to the ground.

Everything was a blur after that. I lay on the ground, fading in and out of consciousness. Every thought left my head, except for the surprising observation that asphalt was more comfortable than I expected.

There was so much noise. I wanted to cup my hands over my ears to block out the repetitive banging sounds, but I couldn't coordinate my arms enough to bring them up by my head.

After an unknown amount of time, with the late morning sun beating down on my back, more hands hauled me to my feet and an arm around my throat kept me standing.

Something cold and hard pressed painfully against my temple.

What was happening?

I thought I heard Brody's voice, but it might have been my hopeful imagination.

Some of my senses came back to me when I was suddenly slammed down into a chair. As I looked around in confusion, several straps were secured across my body, keeping my arms and legs pinned in place.

"Where is Aaron?"

"Wha yu mean?" My slurred words were barely understandable, not even to me. My vision swam when I pried my eyes open, and a masked face loomed over me.

"Aaron Beckham," the same voice demanded, and it took me longer than it should have to realize that the masked person was trying to talk to me. "Where is he?"

"I don't... know." My neck had the strength of a pipe cleaner as I tried to hold up my head, and my chin kept dropping back down to my chest.

BRODY

A hand grabbed my jaw, forcing my head up so I had to look at the masked person.

"Don't play with me. Where is Aaron Beckham?"

Aaron Beckham?

I knew that name. I couldn't match a face to the name, but the sound of it reached down into my chest and a sob bubbled up my throat. Tears dripped unbidden from my eyes and carved hot paths down my cheeks. I didn't even know why I was crying, but I couldn't make myself stop.

Another masked person shoved the first one aside and grabbed the front of my shirt, shaking me so that my back repeatedly slammed against the chair I was bound to.

"Stop blubbering and tell us where he is. That thief is going to pay, and if you don't cooperate, then you'll be joining him."

I barely heard what they were saying. That familiar but unknown name was still bouncing around inside my head, echoing in my ears and blocking out all other sounds. I didn't even realize we were in a vehicle until everything suddenly swerved to the side.

"What the—" The person holding me had to brace against the side of the van to keep from toppling over. "What the hell are you doing up there?"

All three of the people in the back of the van with me looked toward the front where another masked individual sat behind the wheel.

"That ginger bastard is chasing us."

"What?" Three faces peered out of the van's small windows, all jostling for a better view. It was such a ridiculous sight that I couldn't help laughing.

Laughing and still crying at the same time. I must have looked like a lunatic.

One of the masked people jumped into

the front of the van to lean out the window and started shooting a gun behind us. The whole van swerved again, even more drastically than before. People stumbled and shouted as they were thrown around.

Ironically, the straps meant to imprison me actually kept me secure in my seat.

The sound of a second gun joined the fray, then the whole van shook violently. We swerved so hard that everyone still standing was knocked off their feet and even the driver struggled to hang onto the wheel.

Someone shouted "Oh, shit!"

The whole van spun.

I had just enough time to register the pain as my head knocked against something, then everything went black.

***

"What do you mean I can't file a Missing

Persons report?" I demanded from the officer sitting at the front desk. "My brother is missing. I need you to help find him. Why aren't you doing anything?"

The officer sighed, not even looking up from her paperwork as she answered me.

"Mister Beckham. This is your third time here trying to file a report, and we've told you the same thing every time. For a Missing Persons report to be filed, the person has to be missing."

My fist hit the desk hard enough to knock over a cup of pens. "My brother is missing. He's been missing for months, and you're not doing anything to find him."

Very carefully, and with great precision, the officer picked up the cup and replaced each spilled pen one at a time, arranging them in a very specific order.

"Aaron Beckham is not missing. We've contacted him, and he's assured us that he's fine and doesn't need anyone to look for him."

"Contacted him how?" I asked as I watched her arrange all the black pens in a ring around the edge of the cup. "He disappeared without his phone. He's not answering emails. I don't even have an address I can send a letter to."

After the black pens were precisely placed, the officer started forming a second row of blue pens inside the ring of black ones. "If your brother hasn't left you a way to contact him, that is his choice. Nevertheless, we have checked on him, and he's fine."

I ground my teeth together so hard my jaw hurt, and gripped the edge of the table until my fingers turned white. I must have looked like a madman as I stared the officer down, and a few people who were also waiting to approach the front desk scurried away from me.

"He's not fine," I said after I managed

to pry apart my jaw enough to speak. "He just walked away from everything in his life without a word. That's not normal." The officer started to speak, but I cut her off. "Listen. I don't think you understand. My brother has stage four cancer. That's not something a person can just walk away from. He didn't even take his medication with him. He just disappeared. He's probably dying out there somewhere. If you can't file a Missing Persons report, then fine, but just help me get in contact with him so I can make sure he's okay."

Once the blue pens were in place, a new ring of red pens was started. There were only a few, but the officer took extra care to make sure that each red pen sat an equal distance from each other in the ring.

"As much as you may not like it, it's not illegal for a person to walk away from their life. Even taking medication is a choice. What would you have us do? Arrest him? Strap him down and force him to take medication. We've contacted your brother, and he's made it clear that he's fine, everything he's done or not done is his own choice, and he doesn't wish to be bothered. We can't waste any more resources looking for a man who isn't missing."

Talking to these people was like bashing my head against a wall, and I was about ready to start tearing my own hair out. Over the course of several months, I'd visited the police three times. I'd talked to three different officers and tried to argue my case in three different ways.

Each time, it ended up the same way. Being told I couldn't do anything and to stop causing trouble.

Taking a deep breath, I grasped for the last shreds of patience I still possessed. "Aaron may think its his own choice, but its not. He's sick and he's not thinking clearly. He was talking to some questionable people online. I think he was recruited by some cult that's got him convinced they can heal him. If he doesn't take his medication, he'll die. This cult is going to kill him. I'm just trying to save my brother's life. Please. If you can't give me his contact information, can you at least tell me where he is so I can check on him? Surely, that's not too much to ask."

The officer had moved on from the pens and was now organizing the individually unique writing instruments. A highlighter, a white-out pen, and a sharpie were already clustered together in the center of the cup, pressed together by the limited remaining space. The officer paused with a bright green glitter pen in hand, the oversized pompom on the end sticking straight up in the air, and finally looked me in the eye for the first time.

"Mister Beckham. I know this may be

hard to hear, but your brother has not given us permission to tell you where he is or give you any of his information. My advice to you would be to go home, take a good look at yourself, and consider if there is a reason for your brother to cut contact with you."

The last glittery pen was placed securely in the cup, filling the last remaining gap and returning the officer's desk back to its proper order.

I was too furious to even speak. No matter how I tried, no words would come out and I was left gaping at her like an angry fish.

With a wordless shout of frustration, I knocked over her cup and scattered the pens back into a chaotic mess, before storming out of the police station.

I stayed angry all the way back to my apartment. On the public bus, other passengers avoided me, but I hardly noticed as I leaned against the window grumbling under my breath.

How dare that officer imply that I was somehow at fault for my brother's sudden disappearance?

All I'd ever done was support him through his illness. I'd sold my home and moved into this crappy little apartment so that I could help pay off his medical bills. I'd taken care of him when his chemo left him so weak he couldn't get out of bed for days. I'd spent a year living off of mostly instant ramen noodles and tv dinners so that I could afford better quality food for him, cashed in all my vacation and sick days at work so that I could take him to doctor's appointments, and reorganized my entire life around taking care of him.

And then he just walked out the door one day and disappeared.

It wasn't fair. I'd done everything I could to take care of him, yet the officers at the police station looked at me like I was in the wrong. I *must* have done something to drive him away.

My anger persisted until I was back in the little apartment I shared with my brother, sitting on our couch and looking around at the furniture I'd bought for us. The couch was old and sagging, but still comfortable, and the coffee table placed in front of it was only a little slanted.

A pill bottle sat on the table, its bright orange plastic clashing harshly with the brown wood surface.

At the sight of that bottle, all the anger drained out of me and my head collapsed into my hands as I cried.

My brother was sick. He could be dead right now, and I would never know.

Aaron and I had once been very close. We were born barely a year apart, so we'd grown up together and hit most of our milestones around the same time. Even once we were adults, we'd stayed in constant contact. Then, when our parents died, and we were the only family left for each other, we grew even closer. I always thought, no matter what life threw at me, that I'd always at least have Aaron in my corner.

Then he got sick.

At first, he tried to reassure me, saying that people beat cancer all the time. Soon enough, everything would go back to normal, and we'd be able to laugh about it one day.

Yet, that day never came. With each failed treatment, and with each worsening symptom, he grew more and more distant with me, until some days I could barely get two words out of him. He spent most of his time online, talking to people I'd never heard of. These people said ridiculous things, claiming that his cancer was a result of living in a modern city, surrounded by sin and filth every day. That he could be cured if he just returned to the way humans were supposed to live.

I asked Aaron about it once.

What was this way that humans were "supposed to live?"

It was such a vague statement that didn't make sense.

He never answered me.

Then, a few months ago, I went out to refill his prescription, and when I came back the apartment was empty. Aaron took nothing but some cash and his ID with him. His cellphone, his credit cards, even most of his clothes, were all left behind.

That was when I filed the first Missing Persons report and was dismissed by the police for the first time.

I sat on that couch crying for nearly an hour, until finally the tears stopped. At that point, I didn't even care if Aaron refused to come home. I just wanted to know that he was really all right. That he was happy, and his cancer was being treated properly.

I just didn't want to lose the only family I had left.

At some point, while I cried, I'd picked up the medicine bottle and was clutching it so tightly in my hand that the rim of the cap was cutting into my hand.

No, I wouldn't give up. No matter what any officer said, I would keep looking until I knew Aaron was okay.

Or I got confirmation that he was dead.

Another month passed without any sign of my brother. I used the last of my savings to hire a private investigator, but I couldn't afford more than a consultation and a periphery investigation. It was enough to tell me that my brother was probably still alive, as no John Does matching his description had turned up recently, but it still wasn't enough for me to actually find him.

In that time, I was fired from my job for missing too many days of work. I didn't really care. It was just a menial office job that paid barely more than minimum wage. I couldn't stand the place, but without a job I had no money, and without money, I had no means to keep looking for Aaron. Each day looked a little more hopeless, but I still didn't give up.

Then, one evening, I got a text from an unknown number.

It's Aaron. Meet me here.

A map with a pinned location was attached to the message.

It could have been a scam. Most people probably would have questioned such a cryptic message before blindly following its order. However, I was so desperate to find my brother, I never even hesitated. I spent my last few dollars on a bus ticket to a completely different state and headed off that very night.

The pinned location on the map led me to a small town called Rynkirk. The location turned out to be a run down motel on the edge of town. When I arrived, I received another message telling me what room number to go to.

There, lying on the stained motel bed, was my brother.

"Aaron!" I shouted as I ran to him, dropping to my knees beside the bed. It had been months since I last saw him. He'd changed so much that he was barely recognizable. He was once a robust man just like me, but now he resembled a skeleton draped in skin rather than a human. His breathing was shallow and raspy, and when he looked at me, it seemed to take all his effort just to open his eyes.

"Ellis, hey," he greeted me, his voice as rough as sandpaper. "Didn't think you... you'd actually show up."

"Of course I showed up." I gripped his hand and nearly jumped at how cold it was. "I've been looking everywhere for you. I was so worried. You just disappeared and I... I..."

Aaron squeezed my hand. There was barely any pressure to it, but he seemed to be putting everything he had into that grip. "I know. I messed up. I was so stupid. I never should have listened to them, but I was just so scared. Nothing was working. I was dying, and I didn't... I didn't want to die."

"You're not going to die," I insisted, but he cut me off with a weak shake of his head.

"I am. Don't think I have much time left. Those bastards lied to me until the very end, were probably laughing at me behind my back, but I finally wised up." He smiled, and I could see that his gums had receded around his teeth. "In the end, I'll have the last laugh. Look in the drawer there."

The motel room didn't have much. Just a bed, a small side table with a chair, and an old TV that didn't work. It wasn't hard to figure out what drawer he meant.

Inside, I found a few hundred bucks in cash, and a wooden box with an antique key.

"What is this?" I asked after bringing the box and the cash over to the bed.

"That's my revenge."

Aaron started laughing, but the laugh quickly turned into a cough. He grabbed a tissue from a box sitting on the bed next to him to cover his mouth, and when he pulled it away it was stained with blood. When he finally stopped coughing and his breathing returned to a steadier pace, he tossed the tissue into a nearby trashcan with other bloodied paper.

"I don't have much time left. I'm sorry to put this on you, but I can't just let them get away with it. Take the cash, take the key, and disappear."

"What?" I shook my head, still holding the box with the key. "What do you mean disappear?"

"I mean go somewhere they can't find you," Aaron snapped. The sudden burst of emotion sapped his energy, and he had to take a moment to catch his breath. "I'm sorry. You're confused. Of course you are. I'll explain, but just promise me that you'll hide this key somewhere that no one can ever find it. They'll come looking for you, so you'll have to hide, too. You always liked camping. That might work. Just get a tent, go out into the woods, and stay there."

I stared down at the key, sitting comfortably in its little box. It was definitely an antique, with an intricate design and artistic flower carvings around the handle. It was the kind of key that would be used to unlock something important.

But not more important than my brother's life.

I wanted to argue, to throw away the

key and forget about it, but Aaron was so insistent with his request, there was only one answer I could give. I promised to hide the key, so long as he let me take care of him first.

We stayed in that motel as he explained everything about the key and *The Tamed Souls*. During that time, I took care of him and tried to make him as comfortable as possible.

Two days after I first arrived at the motel, Aaron closed his eyes for the last time.

CHAPTER NINE

Brody

THE BEEPING OF the hospital machines drilled slowly but steadily into my head. I would be hearing that rhythmic high-pitched noise in my dreams for months after this. The clean smell of antiseptic stung my nose, and the temperature was somehow too hot and too cold at the same time.

The only thing worse than the sounds and smells of a hospital was the furniture. Hospital furniture wasn't even comfortable for an average person. For a man my size, sitting on that little plastic chair was akin to one of the punishments of hell.

I deserved it. No matter how uncomfortable I was, and the fact that it wasn't that long of a drive back to Emberwood from Rynkirk, I stayed. Ellis was only in that hospital because of me. I had to stay by his side until he woke up.

It had been nearly twenty-four hours since his attempted kidnapping. Deputy Hillard had been by a few times to tell me about the investigation into the kidnappers and assure me that I wouldn't be brought up on charges. Most of the kidnappers had been killed in the crash, and the few that I had killed myself were clearly self-defense.

I was pretty sure he'd doctored his report about the events. The man I'd killed after the crash had not been a matter of defense. He was already injured and clearly not a threat.

No, I'd killed him out of revenge, but there was no talk about bringing me up on charges for it.

I probably should have asked more questions about the investigation, but I was too focused on Ellis to care.

Why wasn't he waking up?

The doctors had assured me that he had no major injury. The chair that his kidnappers had strapped him to had done an ironically good job of protecting him. He did have a minor concussion, but it shouldn't have kept him unconscious for so long.

The doctors didn't say anything, but I could tell they were worried. Someone not waking up after a head injury, even a minor one, could be a sign of a more serious brain injury.

If only I'd brought him into the diner with me, then all of this could have been avoided. I'd promised to take care of him and keep him safe, and I failed.

How stupid could I be?

No, not stupid.

Selfish.

I'd slept with him, and then out of shame, I'd pushed him away. Now, he was lying unconscious in a hospital bed.

What if he never woke up?

From what I knew about concussions, it was possible.

If that happened, I'd...

I'd...

The ring of my cell phone interrupted me before I could finish that thought.

For a moment, I stared uncomprehendingly at Magnus's name on the screen before my brain snapped back online and I answered it.

"Mag? What is it?"

"Hey, Brody," Magnus said, sounding too casual for the situation. "How... um, how's Ellis?"

My gaze flickered toward the

monitoring machines again, showing the steady rhythm of Ellis's pulse. "Nothing's changed since the last time you asked me an hour ago. Now, get to the point. You wouldn't have called just for that."

"Okay. Rude. But you're right. I've... I've found out some information about Creed."

I hadn't forgotten about the situation with Creed, but in all the chaos happening with Ellis it had been pushed to the back of my mind.

It seemed I was failing all of my relationships.

"Did they find him?" I asked, hopeful but not optimistic. If Creed had been found, Magnus would have led with that information rather than asking about Ellis again when he knew nothing had changed.

"No, but..." Again, Magnus hesitated, making me more anxious with each silent moment that passed. "They're pretty sure he's POW."

POW.

Prisoner of War.

Every solider had heard this term at least once and spent no small amount of time contemplating the possibility. But it never truly felt real. It was like a boogieman story. It kept us up at night, but under the light of the sun it disappeared to the back of our minds.

Now, the nightmare had caught up to us, and we found that the boogieman was very real.

"Is there—" My voice cracked, and I tried again. "Is there any news about him?"

I could hear Magnus sigh through the phone. "Well, that's the weird part. I was able to find out that Creed was captured, but no one can tell me by who, or even where he is. Hell, they can't even tell me *why* he was captured, but his captors haven't made any demands."

BRODY

No demands?

My heart sank.

People often said that "no news is good news." Whoever came up with that saying had clearly never had someone they cared about go missing. If Creed was captured for the sake of a ransom, that wouldn't be so bad. A ransom could be solved, and it would mean that his kidnappers would had a vested interest in keeping him unharmed.

However, if there was no ransom, then there were only a few reasons why someone would take Creed, and none of those reasons were good.

"I know what you're thinking," Magnus said, just as my thoughts started to spiral into a dark place. "I thought the same thing, but... I don't know. Something about this just isn't adding up. I can't place my finger on why, but this whole situation just feels odd."

"Odd." I huffed out a depressing

imitation of a laugh. "Yeah. You can say that again."

Movement on the hospital bed caught my attention. Ellis stirred, his eyelids fluttering as he tried to open his eyes, and he grasped at the thin sheet covering most of his body, fisting it in his hands.

"Hey, Mag. I'll have to call you back. Let me know if you find anything else out."

"Yeah. Will do."

With a quiet beep the line went dead, and I shoved the phone back in my pocket just as Ellis finally opened his eyes.

He turned his head, looking straight at me like he knew I'd be there. His dark eyes were like black holes sucking in all the light. They drew me in until I was sitting forward on the edge of my uncomfortable little chair.

"Beckham," he said, so quiet I had to ask him to repeat himself. "Ellis Beckham. That's my name."

BRODY

He blinked and light flickered through his eyes. The empty black holes became a night sky filled with stars. All at once, he sat up, dislodging one of the monitors connected to him and causing the machines to start beeping. Yet, he didn't even notice the noise as he grabbed my hand.

"Ellis Beckham. I'm Ellis Beckham. I remember everything. I remember..."

Just as quickly as he grabbed me, he suddenly froze. The light that had glittered so joyously in his eyes dimmed and was replaced by beautiful but horrifying tears.

"I remember everything. Oh God. Aaron. He... I..."

With each word his voice died a little more until he couldn't utter a sound.

Yesterday, I'd been convinced that keeping as much distance between Ellis and myself was the best choice. An hour ago, I was questioning that decision, but I still wasn't convinced that getting involved with him was the right thing to do.

The sound of his sobs broke me.

Seeing him sitting there on that too small hospital bed, body heaving as he cried into the shelter of his own hands, what else could I do?

I squeezed myself onto the edge of the bed, wrapped my arm around his shoulder, and held him close as he cried. I had no idea what he'd remembered that upset him so much, but it didn't matter. I didn't need to know the meaning behind his tears to comfort him through them.

Eventually, he managed to calm down enough to talk, though the tears kept trickling from his eyes. He told me about his older brother, who'd been fighting a losing battle against cancer until a cult seduced him away with fake promises. Then, in his final days, Aaron had returned, with an antique key in hand and a tall order for Ellis to fulfill.

"He made me promise not to bother with a proper burial," Ellis said after blowing his nose for the dozenth time. "There wasn't time. These—what were they called? *The Tamed Souls?*—These Tamed Soul bastards were coming after me for the key that Aaron stole. He wanted me to just leave him in the motel for the police to eventually find, but I couldn't just abandon his body like that. I wrapped it up in some sheets and found a peaceful spot in the woods to bury him. He was right. I shouldn't have taken the time. That's why the cult managed to catch up to me. I managed to escape, but I knew they were right behind me. So, I hid the key just in case I was caught and headed up into the mountains to hide out as long as I could."

"And then I dropped a tree on you," I concluded. Even though he'd stopped crying, I kept my arms wrapped around him. I couldn't deny how good it felt to hold him close. "I'm glad you got your memories back, and that your name really is Ellis. It would be weird to find out I'd been calling you by the wrong name all this time."

"I wouldn't mind any name you wanted to call me."

It was obvious he spoke without thinking. His face was half-buried against the hollow of my shoulder, and I could feel the heat from his blush even through my shirt. My first instinct was to laugh it off and pretend he'd said nothing. It was so much easier to ignore things and avoid uncomfortable conversations.

But I couldn't do that to him. I'd already messed up so much with him, it was time to step up and take responsibility.

"Ellis," I began, not really sure where I was going with this. "Now that you've got your memories back, does that... does that change anything?"

BRODY

He sat up enough to look at me. His hair was mussed up from sleeping for so long and stuck out in all directions.

"Change anything?" he asked. He must have noticed the direction of my gaze, for he started running his hands through his hair to try and tame the wild curls.

He only ended up making them worse, and I had to fight the urge to reach out and fix his hair for him.

"Yeah, like, should I be looking over my shoulder for a jealous husband or boyfriend that might want to take revenge on me?"

It was the first time I'd openly acknowledged what had transpired between us since the night it happened. The look of excitement and hope that lit up Ellis's face made my stomach churn with even more guilt.

I really had fucked this up. No one should look that happy while sitting injured in a hospital bed.

"No, there's no one," he quickly assured me. "No husband or boyfriend. Not even any friends, really."

He tried to laugh as if that last statement were a joke, but he couldn't hide the obvious hurt in his voice or the way his words wobbled like they would fall apart at any minute.

"I mean, I did have friends. Once. But, when my brother got sick, taking care of him took all my time, and I found out that the people I thought were my friends were..."

Although he couldn't seem to find the right explanation, I understood what he was trying to say.

"Fairweather friends?"

"Yes, exactly. Once I got busy and wasn't *fun to be around* anymore, well, they stopped being around me. Honestly, I'm jealous of the relationship you have with Magnus. You guys are real friends. I don't think I've ever known anything genuine like that, except maybe my brother, but he left me in the end as well. I think... maybe, I'm just not cut out for real relationships."

"Hey, that's not true."

I tightened my grip on him. It probably hurt, but he didn't try to pull away, and even leaned closer to me.

"Then, why don't you..."

There were so many ways he could have finished that question, and none of them would be pleasant, but he never got the chance. At that moment, a nurse stepped through the door and our conversation ended.

"I see someone's finally awake," the nurse said as she closed the door to the private room behind her. "We've all been very worried about you. Your partner here has barely left your side."

Ellis and I both opened our mouths like we were about to correct her, then simultaneously chose to remain silent.

The nurse finally switched off the wailing machine and reattached the monitor that had come loose from Ellis when he woke up. Blessed silence reigned for a moment, but it was quickly interrupted as the nurse started asking Ellis a series of rapid-fire questions to determine how he was doing.

After his earlier breakdown, he was still very dazed, and mostly gave the nurse halfhearted or vague answers. This didn't seem to bother her, as she marked everything down on the chart, and assured him that some confusion was normal after being unconscious for over a day, but to let someone know if the symptom persisted.

I suspected his disorientation was a result of the emotional roller coaster he'd been on in the last twenty-four hours rather than a result of his concussion, but I didn't correct the nurse. This was her job, and I wasn't going to tell her what to do.

It was, however, good to hear that Ellis didn't seem to be suffering from any negative effects of the accident. He'd been incredibly lucky that he'd been secured to such a sturdy chair when the van overturned. It had kept him mostly safe and allowed him to avoid any serious injuries. As much as I hated feeling grateful to his kidnappers, I was very glad that they'd chosen to restrain him so thoroughly.

Eventually, after nearly an hour of poking and prodding, the nurse finally left. Ellis and I were left staring awkwardly at each other, unsure how to pick up the threads of our interrupted conversation.

"Listen..." Ellis sighed as he chose to break the silence first. "I'm not expecting anything. I don't want you to feel obligated—"

"Stop," I cut him off, reaching out to

grab his hand. I'd moved off the bed to give the nurse space to work, and I was already hating the extra distance between us. "This isn't about expectations or obligations."

Ellis pulled his hand away from me. "Isn't it? You took me in because you felt responsible for me after I lost my memories. You protected me because you thought that those cult members were after you and that I was just caught in the crossfire. Everything between us has been out of obligation. And, you know, I get it. I don't bring anything to the table. No money. No friends or family. No job. I got my memories back, but it makes no difference. I have no life worth remembering. So, I'm not surprised that you're here out of obligation. There's no other reason for you to get involved with me."

He obviously had even more to say, but I'd already heard enough. Before he could utter another word, I leaned over and pressed my mouth to his.

At first, I expected him to fight me. He'd been so determined to pull away from me, and a kiss definitely crossed more lines than just holding his hand.

Yet, the moment our lips touched, he melted against me like he was a block of ice that had been shoved directly into a bonfire.

Without breaking the kiss, I moved back onto the bed until I was pressed up right next to him. Logically, I knew it wasn't the best kiss. His breath was stale from his long sleep, I hadn't shaved in several days, and Ellis's cheeks were still red and his eyes rimmed from his earlier tears.

It was also the sweetest kiss I'd ever experienced. I would have happily stayed there, squished onto the little hospital bed as I wrapped myself around him, and kissed him for the rest of my natural life.

Unfortunately, biology wasn't so kind, and we soon had to part in order to catch our breaths.

"It was never about obligation," I said as I leaned my forehead against his. "I took care of you because I wanted to. I protected you because I wanted to. And... I slept with you because I wanted to. I only pushed you away afterward because I thought I was protecting you. I thought I was doing the right thing and that taking care of you was more important than my own desires, but all I did was hurt you. That was my mistake, but I'm not going to make the same mistake again. I want you. Plain and simple."

Ellis grabbed onto the front of my shirt and brought us back together for another kiss, just as sweet as the first, although shorter.

"Me too. But I still don't know what I can actually bring to a relationship, or what I'm even looking for. It's been so long since I focused on what I wanted that I don't even know what my own wants even look like anymore."

Bracing my back against the head of the bed, I positioned Ellis so he sat between my legs and could lean back against my chest. It was the only way we could both fit on the small hospital bed, and even then, it was barely comfortable. Especially, since we had to be careful of the multiple wires still connected to him for fear of setting off the machines again.

"I don't know what I'm looking for in a relationship, either. Especially, not right now, with everything going on. How about we take it slow and figure it out one step at a time?"

Ellis settled in easily against my chest, letting his head rest directly over my heart. "Slow sounds good. Although..." He twisted around to look at me with a frown on his face. "Does that mean sex is off the table?"

Instead of immediately replying with words, I first answered him with a kiss. "Oh no. Sex is still on the table. Or the bed. Or the shower. Or wherever you want. I don't think I could keep my hands off you if I tried."

With a smile, he snuggled in closer to me, turning me into his personal pillow. "Good. I could abstain if I had to, but I think that might actually count as torture."

The word *torture* bounced around inside my head like a tennis ball made of barbed wire, pricking everything it touched. For a moment, my thoughts turned to Creed and what he might be going through right now, but I pushed the image away. There was no reason to catastrophize before we even knew what the situation actually was, and it certainly wouldn't help my fragile new relationship with Ellis.

I held him closer. "Yeah. We wouldn't

want that. Nothing but pleasure between us from here on out."

For a moment, it looked like Ellis was about to say something else, but at the last moment he changed his mind and stayed quiet as he returned to his place nestled against me. I found it odd, but didn't give it much more thought as the stress of the last few days finally caught up with me and I dozed off surrounded by the warmth of his body against mine.

***

The hospital staff insisted on keeping Ellis overnight for observation, and then most of the next day was spent going over the results of his final tests—he was surprisingly healthy, considering everything he'd gone through—and then convincing the doctor to finally discharge him.

It was so late when he was finally able to leave the hospital that we probably would have been better off just renting a hotel room for the night and driving back to Emberwood in the morning, but we were too impatient to wait. I hated leaving Magnus alone longer than necessary while there were still people out to get us.

Plus, Ellis was eager to sleep somewhere more comfortable than a hospital bed, and I could attest from personal experience that the beds at Rynkirk's only hotel weren't much better.

At least, that was the excuse he gave for why he didn't want to stay in Rynkirk, but from the way he kept looking back through the rearview mirror as we drove away, I knew there was more to it. This was the city where his brother had died. Somewhere on the outskirts of this town, Aaron Beckham lay in an unmarked grave, completely unknown to the rest of the world. The guilt around his brother's death must be driving Ellis insane, and I didn't blame him for wanting to get some distance from it.

I instinctively moved my hand to rest on his knee, and I squeezed in what I hoped was a comforting gesture. "We'll come back. When this is all over, we'll give your brother a proper burial. I promise."

Laughing quietly to himself, Ellis finally looked away from the rearview mirror and turned his gaze forward. "He'd scold me for feeling guilty. Aaron was always a very practical person. Or, at least, he was until the end. If he could see me now, he'd say I'm being stupid. I did what he asked me to do, so there's no reason to feel guilty about it."

"Well, if emotions were logical, they wouldn't be emotions, would they?"

"Yeah, I guess so." With another sigh, Ellis leaned over and put his head on my shoulder and closed his eyes like it was the most natural thing in the world. "Wake me when we get home."

He was asleep almost instantly, while I was left reeling.

Home?

He'd said it so causally. I'd barely lived there long enough to call it home, and still often caught myself simply referring to it as "the property."

Could Ellis have really gotten comfortable there so quickly that he already considered it home as well?

I should have pushed back against this idea. Every logical thought in my head was saying that it was just a response to the trauma that Ellis had faced recently, and he was simply latching onto the first sense of security that he could find.

But just like I'd told Ellis, emotions weren't logical. So, in spite of all logic, warmth bloomed in my chest as I imagined Ellis making a home in the house I'd built with my own hands.

Driving through the mountains after

dark was dangerous, so when the sun set, I was forced to go much slower than normal. It took nearly twice as long as normal to cover the distance between Rynkirk and Emberwood. By the time I pulled into the gravel parking just in front of my house, it was clear that Magnus and Trent had already turned in for the night. Everything was quiet, and there weren't even any lights on in their house. The whole property was lit by nothing but moonlight, making everything look soft around the edges, like I'd stumbled my way into a dream.

"Hey..." I nudged Ellis, who was still using my shoulder as a pillow. "We're here."

The sleep that clung to his eyes gave him an adorable expression, and I was sad that he woke up so quickly. However, his nap during the drive seemed to have invigorated him, and he practically jumped from the truck with a spring in his step.

"I'm glad nothing's happened to the place while we were gone. I know it may seem weird, but this place has kind of become a safe haven to me, you know."

I wrapped an arm around his shoulder and led him toward the house, always keeping an eye on the tree line. Our home might be a safe haven, but I didn't trust the world beyond our property line.

"I know. Come on. Let's get you inside. You've had a long day."

Ellis seemed more interested in looking around the property than getting inside where it was safe, so I kept my arm around him and practically dragged him along. With his memories restored, he must be revaluating everything with new eyes, so I could understand his distraction. Yet, I couldn't breathe easy until a locked door stood between us and the open night air.

Luckily, Ellis didn't mind coming

inside, for he was just as interested in examining the house as he was the rest of the property.

"Have you considered naming this place?"

I wasn't really listening as I brought him up the stairs, so I just gave him a noncommittal grunt. It hardly counted as a conversation, but my single syllable response was all Ellis needed to keep going.

"You know, like, The Nowhere Ranch, or The Medowshire Estate. Something like that."

My foot hit the top of the stair's landing before I realized what he was saying and turned back to him.

"Wait. What are you talking about?"

Normally, someone would be upset to realize their conversation partner hadn't been listening to them, but Ellis wasn't fazed and kept right on talking with a smile on his face.

"Your property. Places always feel more important when they have an actual name, and your home is so special. It deserves a name as well."

"That's..." I was about to dismiss the idea but stopped when I thought about it for a moment. "That's a good idea. We should do that. Maybe when everything is over, we can figure something out." My gaze landed on the door to the guest bedroom, and I was reminded of even more things that we needed to take care of. "Before that, though, we'll need to track down your stuff. Now that your memories are back, I'm sure you want to get back to your own apartment."

The stairs opened up to the center of the upstairs hallway. One direction led to the master bedroom, and in the other lay the guest bedroom.

Neither of us moved from the stair's landing.

"There's no rush," Ellis said as he

shrugged. "I sold most of my stuff to pay for my brother's treatment, and the apartment I was living in is a shithole. There's literally nothing waiting for me, assuming the landlord hasn't already evicted me for missing rent payments."

He hooked his fingers through the belt loop of my pants. It was such a small gesture, like he was trying to cling to me in the most unobtrusive way possible.

I stared down at his hand, debating the pros and cons of removing his grip.

"We could at least pick up your own clothes, so you don't have to keep wearing mine."

The hand that wasn't clinging to my pants clutched the collar of the shirt he was wearing and pulled it closer to his face. "I kinda like wearing your clothes. They smell like you. It's calming."

The two of us were nearly the same height, but somehow, Ellis still managed to give the impression of looking up at me with an expression that I could only call coy.

"You know, since I have to wear your clothes, getting dressed in the morning would be easier if I woke up in your bed."

Two doors, one decision.

Should I escort him to the guest room, or bring him into my own bed?

I was certain that he would accept either option, though he'd made it clear which he preferred. The decision was entirely up to me.

It didn't take as long as I thought it would to decide.

My bedroom door closed behind us with a resounding slam, like the gavel of a judge's hammer. I wouldn't know until morning if I'd be pleading guilty or walking away innocent, but as I pushed Ellis back toward the bed, I didn't care. His kiss was a thief stealing my every rational thought, and I was a willing victim.

BRODY

Ellis's knees hit the edge of the bed, and I was prepared to push him the final few inches onto my mattress, but before I could, he stopped me with a hand on my chest.

"Wait. Let me..." He paused for a moment, looking down so his gaze was shadowed under his slightly curled lashes. His expression would have looked shy, except for the way he licked his lips. "Let me do something."

He didn't bother waiting for my answer and immediately dropped to his knees. His returned memories had also brought with them a new sense of confidence. Ellis was still the soft, shy man that I'd come to care about, but he was also a man who knew what he wanted. There wasn't a moment of hesitation as he immediately went to work unbuttoning my pants and pulling my straining erecting free from my underwear.

I tangled my hand in his curly hair,

unsure if I wanted to stop him or urge him to continue.

"Are you sure?"

Dark eyes sparkled like the bubbles in a champagne glass, light yet deceptively intoxicating, as he smiled up at me.

"Absolutely."

From that moment, I was doomed.

With a gentle hand, he stroked my cock, driving me wild with tantalizing sensations that were never quite hard enough to satisfy.

My second hand joined my first, and I tightened my grip on his hair. "You... minx," I gasped, squeezing my eyes shut. "You've done this before."

His mouth hovered near my arousal without making contact, just close enough for me to faintly feel the breath of his laughter. "I'm forty-five. Did you really think I was a virgin?"

"No, but—"

I choked as he sped his hand up just a

little bit, and brushed his lips over the sensitive head of my cock.

Ellis laughed again, making my hips buck into the vibrations his voice sent over my skin.

"But you thought I was shy and inexperienced," he concluded for me. "Well, you're not entirely wrong. I am shy. I could never do this with someone I didn't trust. But that doesn't mean I'm an innocent virgin. I know what I want."

With my eyes squeezed shut, I couldn't see his expression, but I could easily picture the way he must be looking up at me with hunger. The implication of his words was obvious. He knew what he wanted, and it was me.

In one smooth move, he parted his lips and swallowed me whole.

He was definitely experienced. I'd even go so far as to say he was a slut, in all the best ways. He moved his mouth and tongue over me with the precision of an expert musician playing their favorite instrument. Completely new sounds were dragged out of me. Sounds I didn't even know I could make. I gasped and howled when my cock hit the back of his throat and kept going. Either he didn't have a gag reflex or he'd perfected the ability to suppress it as he easily deepthroated me.

Every nerve in my body came alive at the same time. My legs shook and I was in danger of toppling forward. Luckily, Ellis had a solid figure. I braced one hand against his shoulders to keep myself upright and held on for dear life.

He pulled away slowly, letting his tongue dance along the underside of my cock until only the head remained between his lips. Then he swallowed me again, alighting my pleasure all over again. Each time was like the strike of a blacksmith's hammer in my mind. My climax was forged one thunderous spark at a time until I couldn't hold back no matter how hard I tried. I gleefully let myself tumble over that edge, driving myself as deep down his throat as possible.

Ellis didn't try to push me away, didn't even seem to struggle, as he eagerly swallowed every drop of my pleasure.

By the end, I was left panting and shaking. Ellis pulled off of me, but remained kneeling at my feet so I could continue using him for support until I calmed down enough to stand on my own.

Breathing deeply through my nose, I willed my pulse to slow. I refused to be a selfish lover. I'd found my release, but arousal still strained against Ellis's pants and his eyes still burned with need.

"Come here," I said as I pulled him to his feet. "My turn to take care of you now."

I slid my hand under his shirt, popping open the buttons one at a time until his entire torso was bare. Black hair stood out starkly on his olive skin, and the soft curve of his belly fit perfectly against my palm. I squeezed the love handles that spilled out over the tops of his borrowed jeans and reveled in the soft yet sturdy feel of him.

I was so ready to dive right into him. Despite having just come, my cock was already twitching with interest again. It wouldn't be long before I was ready for a second round, but this time I was going to make sure it was all about his pleasure instead.

I didn't realize I'd spoken that last thought out loud until I noticed Ellis giving me a strange expression.

"Do you really want to make me feel good?"

His lashes fluttered, and he couldn't quite meet my eye. He looked nervous, though I had no idea why that would be. Surely, after getting on his knees for me, there was nothing left for him to be nervous about.

"Of course." Grabbing his hand, I placed a kiss against his knuckles. "You deserve all the pleasure I can give you."

Biting his lip, Ellis hesitated for a moment, then leaned forward to whisper directly in my ear.

My brain stalled and the whole world around me seemed to freeze as I processed his unexpected request.

CHAPTER TEN

Ellis

"YOU WANT ME to... what?" Brody looked at me with an unreadable expression.

My momentary confidence wavered, and I stared down at the floor beneath my bare feet.

"I just... thought it would be something you'd like."

"I'd like?"

Brody's face was already flushed from my earlier attentions, but I swear it got redder as he gave me a knowing look and tipped my chin up to meet his gaze.

"You asked me to tie you to the bed. I don't think this is about what I'd like. I think this is your interest. Tell me. With your memories back, have you also remembered your own... interests?"

I couldn't answer. My throat felt like it was being constricted by an iron hand, even as the taste of him still lingered on my tongue. With my face burning and my breath coming in erratic little pants, I nodded.

Fear and excitement raced through me at the same time. I was terrified that Brody would reject me. That I'd pushed too far and now he was disgusted with me. Yet, also brought with it a thrill. I'd taken a risk and put myself out there. I was as vulnerable as I could be, without actually being tied up, and I had no idea what would happen.

The anticipation made my blood run hotter with each moment that passed as I waited for Brody to answer.

His hand rested light on my chest, just over my heart. It was an incredibly tender gesture, at odds with the heat of the moment.

"Explain it to me," he eventually said. "I'm not saying no, but I'm also not going to say yes until I know exactly what you're expecting. There's been enough miscommunication between us. I don't want any more."

"I want..." My vocal cords twisted into a knot, and I couldn't get the words out. I swallowed hard, trying to free up my voice, and I felt the heat of Brody's gaze as he watched the motion. "I want you to make me feel like I belong to you. Like I'm yours to do whatever you want with. I want... I want..."

"You want to be made to submit," he finished for me.

My words failed me again, so I just nodded.

"I'm guessing you don't get many opportunities for that sort of role." His gaze traveled up and down my body, and I knew exactly what he was talking about. Somehow, the fact that Brody already understood before I'd even managed to speak it out loud made the words easier to say.

I laughed with a sad little puff of air. "Yeah. Anytime I suggest any sort of powerplay in bed, people always take one look at me and assume I want to be dominant. It's hard to convince them otherwise. I mean, I get it. I'm not the pretty little twink you usually picture when you think of a submissive, but..."

I sighed, and my first instinct was to just say we should forget I'd ever suggested anything. However, I steeled my nerves and tried one last time, looking Brody directly in the eye with all the confidence I had.

"Just once I wish I didn't have to

defend myself. That when I told my partner my preferences, they'd just believe me, and that they'd want the same thing. And... and I was hoping you'd be that person."

The hand on my chest slid higher until it rested on my collarbone, just under my throat.

"So, you want me to pin you down and own you."

While technically a question, he said it with the certainty of a statement.

Swallowing again and holding my breath in anticipation, I nodded.

He moved his hand higher until it wrapped around my throat.

"I can do that."

Just for a moment, his grip tightened, cutting off my air. Then, he shoved me backward, so I fell onto the bed. I barely had time to brace myself and keep track of my sprawling limbs before he was on me.

The last of our clothing was ripped away and tossed across the room where it was immediately forgotten. It was a warm night, but I still shivered under Brody's gaze.

"Not getting overwhelmed already, are you?" he asked as he ran a hand down my side.

I responded by arching my back enough to grind our hips together.

He chuckled under his breath, creating a deep sound that made all the hair on my body stand on end. "I'll take that as a *no*. Now, be patient. I need to get some stuff."

I assumed I knew what he needed to get. We'd had sex in this bed before, and I'd already seen him fetch condoms and lube from the nightstand before. So, I was surprised when instead of simply reaching over for the nearby drawer, he stood from the bed and completely left the room.

BRODY

Sitting on the bed, I was left there, stunned. For a moment, there was nothing but silence and I assumed he'd come right back. Then, faintly, I heard the sound of the back door opening.

Brody was completely naked. He couldn't have left the house. Although, it was his property, and there were no neighbors to spy on him, so I supposed he could do whatever he wanted.

But why?

He seemed eager for what we were about to do. Surely, he hadn't gotten cold feet and left me.

I debated going after him, counting the moments in my head until his return. When nearly a minute passed, I began to grow nervous and wandered toward the bedroom door.

My hand was almost on the handle when it suddenly opened. Luckily it swung away from me, otherwise it would have smacked me right in the face.

Brody stood in the doorway, nearly filling the entire space and trapping me inside the room without even trying. In his hand, he held a length of cotton rope.

"Getting impatient already?" he asked as he wound the rope around his hand as if testing its strength. "I told you to be patient."

My eyes tracked the movement of the rope. It creaked a bit when pulled taught, and the sound made something deep in my gut clench with anticipation. "You were gone for a while."

He gave the rope an extra twist, emphasizing the soft sound it made. "Took me longer to find this than I thought. But still..." He let go of the rope with one hand and reached up to cup my cheek. "When I tell you to be patient, I expect you to listen."

Then he suddenly grabbed my shoulder and spun me around so I faced away from him. Then, I was shoved harshly toward the bed. It was rare that I found someone capable of pushing me around so easily. Partners had tried in the past, but they usually just gave up and resorted to verbal orders when my size and weight proved too much for them.

Yet, Brody manhandled me so easily, it felt like my flesh and blood body had suddenly been replaced by paper. I stumbled and barely managed to catch myself on the bed, so I was on my hands and knees on the mattress.

Brody was immediately behind me, his hand on my back keeping me in place. "This is a lovely position, but not quite where I want you."

Firmly but gently, I was rearranged and pushed down onto the mattress until I lay on my front in the center of the bed with my face buried against the blankets. I felt the bed shift as Brody climbed up on the bed as well, letting the full weight of his body settle over me and pin me in place.

"This all right?" he asked, his breath ghosting hot and wet over my ear.

My blood was rushing through my head, and at first, I didn't realize he'd even spoken. After he repeated the question, a little more insistently, I finally managed to gather my wits enough to answer.

"Yeah, it's... it's good. I'm good."

He gave a pleased hum, the vibration tickling my ear and making me squirm.

"Let me know if that changes. If we're going to keep playing like this, we'll have to set up some better ground rules and a safe word. For now, I won't go too hard on you, but just say "switch" if you want me to stop."

"Switch?"

"Like kill-switch.. Basically, it means an emergency stop."

I committed the word to memory, but was also certain I wouldn't need to use it.

BRODY

In that moment, Brody could have done anything to me, and I would eagerly accept.

While Brody kept me pinned under his weight, the cotton rope was wound around my wrists and attached to the headboard. The knots were solid and unyielding, yet not too tight to injure me or cut off circulation.

Still lying on my front, I glanced at Brody over my shoulder. "You've done this before."

His fingers threaded through my hair in an achingly gentle touch, like he was petting something precious and fragile. It was a stark contrast to the sensual tone in his voice as he whispered directly into my ear.

"I took the time to learn a little Shibari on one of my tours when we were stationed in a remote village in Japan. I've played rough before. It was fun, but my partners were never quite... enough to really satisfy, so I usually don't bother suggesting things like this." Slowly, he moved away from my ear and trailed his lips down the skin of my throat. "Think you can handle it?"

His teeth bit into the side of my neck, almost hard enough to draw blood. The sharp burst of pain made me scream, and my hips bucked. The thrashing caused my arousal to rub against the mattress below me, mixing pleasure with the pain.

I moaned when his teeth released me and collapsed against the bed as a tingling sensation danced up and down my spine.

"Yeah, I can take it," I panted. "Please. More. I can definitely take it."

Brody's voice buzzed in my ear, though I was too blissed out to hear his specific words. Just the tone was enough. He was pleased by my answer, but also skeptical. He still wasn't sure if I was telling the truth, and I couldn't blame him for his hesitance. We hadn't known each other that long in the grand scheme of things, but I had one advantage over him.

I had my memories back, and I knew for a fact just how much I could take.

Without warning, Brody's hand came down hard on my ass. It was so sudden that I didn't even feel the pain at first, but as the sound of flesh hitting flesh echoed through the room, my brain caught up with my body. The burn of his strike felt like it reached right down into my core and ignited a flame inside me. I moaned and angled my body to press back against his hand, trying to get more contact.

Brody carefully stroked the area he'd just struck, acting as though he were soothing my bruised flesh when really, he was just aggravating the already angry nerve endings.

"Maybe you can take it," he mumbled before pinching that same spot.

I was going to have an impressive

bruise on my ass when he was done, and we'd barely started.

My tongue already felt like it was tied in knots, so I didn't bother trying to respond. I just buried my face against the mattress and nodded. I felt Brody moving around behind me but couldn't see what he was doing. The only clue I had was his distracted mumbling.

"Too bad we didn't plan ahead. With more time to prep, I could do so much more with you. Oh well. This'll be enough for now."

Enough?

He wasn't' stopping was he?

I got my answer soon enough. Using his knees, he spread my legs farther apart, and with one hand on the small of my back to keep me still, he roughly slid a lubed finger inside me.

Compared to the pain that still lingered around the abused spot on my ass, the stretch of one finger inside me was almost unnoticeable. Even the jolt of cold lube against my hot skin was more noticeable. I didn't say anything, but Brody immediately picked up on my lack of response, and a second finger joined the first.

He slid his fingers in and out of me, scissoring them apart and stretching me open while the hand on my back still kept me pinned. I felt his weight shift as he leaned forward until his breath brushed against the tip of my ear.

The fingers inside me jabbed at a particularly sensitive spot, while at the same time he bit down on the other side of my neck. Pain and pleasure were indistinguishable. Everything melted together into one intense moment of feeling. I didn't even realize I was screaming until I felt the hoarse tickle in my throat.

He continued to drive his fingers in and out of me, hitting my most pleasurable spot every time. Each thrust didn't come with another bite, but he did tangle one hand tightly into my hair to keep my head pressed down against the mattress, and the tugging left a constant tingle along my scalp.

I lost myself in the sensation and panted so hard that the sheets beneath my face grew wet with spit. The knot in my gut twisted tighter and tighter, pushing me toward an end that I both feared and longed for.

Then, all at once, everything stopped.

"Not so fast," Brody said before nipping the shell of my ear. "We aren't done. I'm not even inside you yet."

His fingers inside me disappeared, and even the hand tangled in my hair pulled away. The sudden loss of sensation left me reeling. I was desperate to get him back and tried to chase after him, only to be reminded of my bound wrists.

Tugging at the ropes hard enough to

shake the headboard, I begged as tears dripped from my eyes.

"Please. Wait. No. Come back. I need… I need more."

It wasn't long until his weight was pressing down on me again, spreading my legs wide enough to accommodate his hips, but even that short time was too much. I practically sighed in relief when I felt the hard shaft of his cock sliding against my bruised ass. While I'd been panicking, he'd prepared himself with a condom and more lube, meaning he wasn't going to hesitate much longer.

Any moment now, I'd finally be satisfied.

That moment came almost immediately, and yet it was still too slow.

Grabbing onto both my shoulders, Brody lined himself up and thrust inside me. I felt every inch of him as my inner muscles stretch to accommodate him, but it wasn't enough.

I needed more.

Harder.

Faster.

When he was only about halfway inside, I gripped onto the headboard and used the leverage to thrust my hips back into him, slamming him the rest of the way home all at once.

We both groaned in unison. Brody dug his fingers into the meat of my shoulder as he clung tightly to me, adding more bruises to the already impressive series of marks he'd left decorating my skin.

He was rough, almost uncaring, as he pulled most of the way out and shoved in again. Each thrust shoved me down hard against the bed, driving the air from my lungs until I could barely breathe. Black spots danced across my vision. I could barely move. Even my fingers didn't want to respond and could only meekly cling to the headboard.

It was ecstasy and oblivion all at once.

Hot tears rolled down my cheeks as I gave in to the overwhelming sensations and suffered joyously inside my own skin.

"You're crying now?" Brody panted as he rutted into me.

There wasn't enough air in my lungs to speak. I could barely even nod, but I managed to jerk my head just enough to get the meaning across.

He thrust in hard again, even deeper than before. "Good. You fucking asked for this. So, take it."

As he continued pounding into me, he buried his teeth in my flesh again. The sting was never enough to indicate that he drew blood, but it was a close call. He littered bite marks all across my neck, shoulders, and even part of my back. Anywhere his mouth could reach was fair game, and I gave it all to him. There wasn't an inch of my body that I tried to hide.

The faster he went, the slower my

thoughts became, until the only thing inside my head was a gray mist. I floated between the line of pleasure and pain like driftwood on the ocean, helplessly going wherever the current took me.

Time passed slowly, yet before I knew it, Brody was speeding up even harder and faster inside me. I could tell he was close, and while I didn't want it to end, I also didn't want him to hold back.

Brody wrapped his hand around me to grip my cock and started stroking me in time to his thrusting. My whole body tensed, clenching down around him. The pleasure in my gut, which had slowly been coiling tighter and tighter, abruptly sprang loose. I came with a shout that was muffled against the pillow, spilling my release across the lines of his fingers.

At the same time, Brody grabbed onto the headboard with his other hand for extra leverage, thrust deeper inside than he ever had before, and followed me into his own climax.

I couldn't have described the moment to save my life. Words like pleasure and ecstasy weren't enough. Bliss was an accurate term, but it was also too soft. The feelings that passed between us weren't soft. They were rough and aggressive, like the heat of burning gunpowder igniting inside a gun. My release had hit me with the force of a bullet, equal parts pain and pleasure, and I couldn't have been happier about it.

When the intense sensations finally let us go, Brody collapsed on top of me. If I'd been any smaller, I would have been completely crushed. Even now, my shoulders felt the strain as my arms remained tied to the headboard, and my lungs struggled to draw in a much-needed breath.

"Oh, sorry," Brody said when he noticed my gasping and quickly raised himself off of me. "Hold on. Let me get that."

I hadn't paid attention to what kind of knot he'd used to secure the ropes around my wrists, other than noticing that they were tight. However, they must have been expertly tied, because despite how securely they held me, the knots easily came free when Brody tugged on them in just the right way.

My arms landed like limp string on the mattress beside my head. I tried to thank him, but the only sound that came out of me was a useless little grunt.

Brody just laughed. "You're welcome." He sounded nearly as tired as I felt, but still managed to raise himself off the bed. "Hold on for a second. I'll get you cleaned up."

Time no longer mattered. He could have been gone for seconds or hours as I lay there, face down and utterly spent. Eventually, he returned, and a warm washcloth was dragged along my skin.

BRODY

The soft material soothed my hurts, and soon enough, I was left with only the ache of a very pleasant evening.

Everything hurt in the best way. I hadn't been so thoroughly fucked since before my brother got sick, and I hadn't realized how much I missed it. Not just the sex, but the mindless oblivion that came afterward. My mind was quiet, and my body lay completely still.

Without realizing it, I dozed off under Brody's gentle care.

***

Sunlight streamed through the window at a much steeper angle than I expected when I woke up. As soon as rational thought returned to me, the first thing my gaze did was jump to the nearby clock.

It was nearly noon.

The bed beside me was cold, but there was a distinct impression among the sheet where Brody had slept, so I knew I hadn't been abandoned the previous night. Brody was a man of action. He couldn't just sit there while he waited for me to wake up and was no doubt working on some project around the property.

They really needed to come up with a name for the place. Calling it "The Property" even in my own head was annoying.

It was comforting to trust someone enough to know that even if I couldn't see them, they were still around. With all of my previous friends, partners, and even my brother, there was always a lingering fear that they would disappear the moment I took my eyes off them. I'd assumed it was my own anxiety that caused such feelings, but I was beginning to realize that the fear stemmed from the fact that I never trusted them. I never felt valued and was left wondering if each time we parted was the last time they'd bother reaching out to me.

BRODY

Brody was different. From the first moment we met, I knew I could rely on him. He made it clear that he never did anything he didn't want to do, so if he was spending time with me it was because he wanted my presence in his life.

Even after such a short amount of time, looking through Brody's wardrobe for something to wear had already become a familiar routine. Most of his clothing was casual, with only a few more formal pieces. Most looked brand new—some even still had the price tag on them—but I avoided those pieces, nonetheless.

The only formal outfit that had clearly been worn several times before was a military full-dress uniform hidden at the back of the wardrobe. I trailed my fingers over the gold buttons and the collection of various badges pinned to the lapel. I didn't know what they meant, but the sheer number of them was still impressive. I'd have to ask Brody to explain them sometime, so I could fully appreciate his accomplishments.

Maybe I could even convince him to wear the uniform for me sometime.

Letting the uniform go for now, I grabbed a set of clothing that looked like it would fit me and headed for the bathroom. I was immediately greeted by the sight of my own image, and the number of bitemarks and bruises that decorated my skin.

I lost myself for a few minutes just admiring the marks. The worst of the marks still stung when I ran my fingers over them. Brody had come really close to breaking the skin a few times and it would take days for the marks to heal.

I wished they would last forever.

Eventually snapping myself out of my self-exploration, I turned my attention back to my morning routine. A smile came to my face when I saw a brand new toothbrush sitting on the sink right next to Brody's regular one. The fact that Brody had put supplies for me here among his own items rather than storing them in the guest bedroom was a clear sign of my place in this house. I wasn't a guest. I still wasn't sure what exactly we were, but our relationship had definitely passed the casual stage.

After getting dressed, I made my way downstairs to find breakfast already waiting for me on the table.

Well, it was technically lunch, but Brody had chosen to make breakfast food, so it still counted.

"Hey," Brody greeted when I sat at the table across from him. "How're you feeling?"

"Famished," I said as I started piling food onto my plate, grabbing a little of everything he'd prepared.

There were no eggs. He'd made sausage, pancakes, and even fresh-squeezed orange juice, but eggs were clearly missing from the table. They were a standard breakfast food, and I'd seen Brody eating them before, so I knew he liked them.

I, however, hated them, and that was apparently enough reason for Brody to completely forgo serving them at all.

Tipping my head so I was looking up at Brody despite our similar height, I let the collar of my shirt fall open. I had purposely chosen a shirt that was too loose along the shoulders so that more of my bruised skin would be on display, and my effort paid off. Brody's gaze immediately snapped to my neck, and a desire smoldered in his eyes as he stared at the marks he'd left behind.

With one finger, I traced the edge of a bite mark right over my pulse.

"I'm also really sore. I could barely get out of bed."

It was a lie and we both knew it. A few

bruises weren't enough to leave me bedridden, but it was still a fun fantasy.

Brody licked his lips and pushed his chair away from the table. "Maybe you should have breakfast in bed, then."

Before I could answer, the front door burst open and interrupted us.

Magnus strode into the house with long strides, like it was taking all of his control not to run. He made a B-line for the kitchen and slammed his hand on the table hard enough to rattle the dishes.

A few sausage links rolled onto the floor, where the dogs in his wake immediately snatched them up.

"Brody," Magnus practically shouted, oblivious of the dogs at his feet that were stealing our breakfast. "I just heard news about Creed."

A mix of hope and fear spread across Brody's face. "Is he..."

He couldn't even finish the sentence, but his question was clear.

Magnus smiled wide enough to show off a set of dazzlingly white teeth.

"They found him. He's alive."

CHAPTER ELEVEN

Brody

"WHAT DO YOU mean they found Creed?"

Hearing my own voice, it sounded like I was upset by the news. Anyone who didn't know me would have thought I wanted Creed to remain missing. This wasn't true, obviously. I wanted nothing more than for him to be found, but this sudden turn of good fortune was too abrupt, and I couldn't help but feel suspicious.

Magnus threw himself into the chair

across from me at the table, nearly knocking the whole thing over in the process.

"What'd you think I meant? They found him."

Taking a deep breath, I fixed the saltshaker, which had fallen over when Magnus joined us. "Explain."

Beside me, I heard Ellis draw in a sharp breath. He was clearly uncomfortable but refused to say anything. For a moment, I thought there was something wrong between him and Magnus, until I noticed he was staring at the saltshaker still in my hand.

Oh, right.

Wasn't there some superstition about spilling salt?

I'd never bought into such things myself, but Ellis clearly did. So, just to make him happy, I took a pinch of the salt and threw it over my left shoulder.

Ellis immediately relaxed, and he gave

me a grateful smile.

Across the table, Magnus clearly saw the exchange, but chose not to comment on it, focusing instead on the more pressing news about Creed.

"One of my contacts just sent me a message saying that they've managed to locate Creed. He's alive, and as far as they can tell, unharmed."

"As far as they can tell?" I asked.

At that same moment, Trent also came through the open front door, taking the time to close it behind him before joining the rest of us at the table. "Don't get your hopes us too much," he said as he sat down, confirming what I already suspected. "They couldn't give us much information. There was no explanation about what happened to Creed in the first place. They couldn't even confirm that he'd been rescued from his supposed captors. All they said was that he's been located, and that he seems to be all right."

Magnus slumped low in his chair, arms crossed over his broad chest. "At least it's good news. Yesterday, we didn't know if Creed was alive or dead. Now, we know he's okay."

"And I'm happy about that," I insisted, resisting the urge to reach across the table and grab Magnus's hand. I'd leave the physical comfort to Trent. "I'm just going to hold back on celebrating until we know exactly what's going on. But you're right. This is good news. So long as Creed is alive and well, then he'll definitely find a way back to us."

A smirk lit up Magnus's face, bringing back the light in his blue eyes that had momentarily dimmed. "That bastard is probably already working on a plan. If the military hasn't rescued him yet, they better get on it, or he'll take care of the job himself."

I nodded along. "It wouldn't surprise me if getting captured was all part of some plan of his to begin with."

I said it as a joke, and we both laughed, but the more I thought about it, the more I began to wonder.

Could Creed have orchestrated his own capture?

Well, yes. It made an odd kind of sense. Creed was the most cunning and the most ruthless of all of us. Survival was a special skill of his, which he had honed down to an art. In all the years we'd served together, I could only think of a few times where he'd ended up in legitimate danger, and those instances had always been cleanly handled by the end.

Suddenly getting captured was so out of character for him. However, the thought of him orchestrating it on his own actually made more sense.

But why?

What would he stand to gain from such a deception?

We'd never know for sure until we asked him, and even under the best circumstances it would be several months before we saw him face to face again.

A rhythmic tapping of metal against wood caught my attention.

Ellis sat beside me, half listening to the conversation and half lost in thought, while idly tapping a painfully familiar key against the table.

Despite clearly being distracted by his own thoughts, he immediately noticed when he had my attention. Looking down at his hands, he realized what he was doing and shoved them in the pockets of the hoodie he'd borrowed from me, hiding the key out of sight at the same time.

"Sorry. Didn't mean to interrupt."

"No, it's all right," I insisted, cursing myself for putting such an ashamed look on his face. "I just didn't realize you still had Poppy Milford's key. I thought we'd locked that away."

"Oh." Hesitantly he took the key back out of his pocket, placing it on the table in front of him without ever letting it go. "It was put away, but I got it out again. I know it's silly, but this key is the last thing my brother gave me. It feels tied to him, so I just like holding onto it. I hope that's okay."

Grabbing the key and his hands all at once, I curled his fingers around the slightly warm metal and pushed it back toward him. "Yeah. It's fine. Given the situation, I'd say you have just as much right to it as anyone."

Clutching the key close, Ellis turned it over and over in his hands so the light from the window caught on the subtle floral design carved into the handle.

"You know, the sad thing is, I don't think my brother even knew what this key was for. He just knew it was important to those *Tamed Souls* people. The only reason he took it was to get back at the cult that deceived him with false promises. He could have gotten back at them in a dozen different ways, but he chose to steal the one thing that ended up leading me here. It all feels so... fated."

I kept my reaction to his words under strict control, not wanting to offend him. I didn't believe in fate, but if that thought gave Ellis comfort then I wasn't going to take it away from him.

Magnus, however, had no reason to hide his own reaction. He snorted with obvious disdain and leaned back on the legs of his chair far enough to make the wood creak.

"I wouldn't bother talking about fate until we know what that key is for. It could turn out to be a red herring for all we know."

Trent laid a hand on his thigh, pressing downward until Magnus had to bring the front legs of his chair back to the floor. "Considering you found that key hidden in a coffin that was buried on your property, I doubt it's meant to be a trick. Red herrings are usually easy to find. That's their point."

Magnus scoffed again, but he sat a little straighter and let his hand rest over Trent's. "A coffin that held a body we still haven't identified. Wouldn't it be ironic if the body turned out to just be some unimportant John Doe, and this whole thing has been a wild goose chase."

While I didn't believe in fate, I also knew better than to issue such a challenge to the universe as Magnus just had. Usually, such challenges would be beneath the universe's notice. However, every now and then, when a challenge was issued, the universe would answer.

Today was one of those lucky days.

Mere moments after Magnus finished speaking, with his breath probably still lingering in the air around him, the ground beneath our feet started to shake.

I instinctively grabbed Ellis, while across from me Magnus did the same with Trent.

Was this an earthquake?

I'd never been through one before, but it didn't seem right. I could hear something moving outside, like crumbling rock, and the tremors were coming from mostly one direction.

The earthquake—or whatever it was—didn't last long, but it made a horrendous noise and seemed in danger of shaking my house right off its foundation. I'd built the place with my own hands, and if I'd cut corners anywhere it probably would have collapsed.

Under different circumstances, I would have gloated over the strength of my construction. When the shaking finally stopped, my house was barely affected except for a few items that had fallen off the shelves. Unfortunately, pride was the furthest thing from my mind as I slowly removed myself from the protective shield I'd formed around Ellis.

"What the hell was that?"

Magnus also stood up slowly, helping Trent to his feet as well. "That wasn't an earthquake. I think... something happened outside."

Something had happened, all right. We didn't have to do more than open the front door and step out onto the porch to get our answer.

A wide chasm had opened up in the ground just behind Magnus's house. It was the exact same spot where Magnus had dug up the coffin. He'd been planning on putting a greenhouse there, but now, instead of a crumbling old concrete slab, there was now a gaping hole straight down into the earth.

"What the hell?" Magnus shouted, stumbling a few feet toward the hole before Trent stopped him.

I silently agreed with Magnus,

although my own feet stayed rooted to the floor of the porch.

What the hell?

A surprisingly soft touch to my arm startled me out of my shock as Ellis clung to my arm.

"Should we... I don't know, call someone?"

His dark eyes looked toward me, expecting me to have the answer.

I didn't. I had no idea what was going on. All I could do was solve the problem the way I always did. By charging forward.

"Wait here." I removed his hands from me, squeezing them for a moment in a show of comfort, before stepping off the porch and heading for the newly opened hole in the ground.

"Are you sure that safe?" Trent called out, still holding back Magnus from following me.

"I won't get too close," I called back

over my shoulder. "I just want to try and see what happened."

The ground felt solid under my feet as I approached. If it weren't for the big hole right in front of me, the land would have seemed exactly the same as it was a few minutes ago.

The closer I got, the more I could tell that the hole wasn't as big as I first thought. Its sudden appearance had made it seem massive enough to swallow Magnus's entire house, but it was actually only about ten or fifteen feet across. The most concerning thing was the fact that it was on our property, and so close to our houses. Out in the middle of the forest, a chasm of this size wouldn't have been worth a second thought.

This new observation gave me the confidence to step a little closer, still on the lookout for any more unstable land. I was only a few feet away from the edge when I discovered that the hole also wasn't as deep as I thought. The walls of the hole were only a little taller than me. I could easily climb down without hurting myself.

Finally at the very edge, I could see the entire floor of the pit. There wasn't as much rubble from the collapsing land as I expected, and the floor was surprisingly flat.

Almost as if it had been made that way.

My philosophy in life was to keep charging forward. It was how I survived the most grueling moments on the battlefield, and it was how I would get my answers now.

Not waiting another moment to second guess myself, I took hold of the edge of the hole and lowered myself down.

"Brody!" Several voices shouted at once, but I was already out of sight. I saw nothing but exposed soil and rock as I hung from the edge of the hole. Even with my arms extended as far as they would go, my feet didn't quite reach the ground.

With a small, but potentially dangerous leap of faith, I let go of the edge.

My feet hit the ground almost immediately, and just as I thought, it was perfectly stable. I didn't even stumble when I landed.

Looking up, I found three worried faces staring down at me.

"I'm fine," I waved to them.

Ellis and Trent both looked relieved, but Magnus's worry turned to anger.

"Fuck off. Don't you dare scare me like that. I thought you just jumped to your death."

His accusations almost made me feel insulted.

"I'm not that stupid," I insisted, though the look on Magnus's face said he wasn't convinced. "I noticed something about this pit and wanted to take a closer look."

Running a hand over the wall of the hole, I found it smooth and straight. Earth didn't crumble in such perfect lines.

"This isn't natural," I called up to the others. "This hole was built."

One side of the hole had a lot more debris than the other. I started shifting it out of the way, moving aside large stones that were also too perfectly shaped to be natural. Behind me, I heard whispered voices, followed by a shifting of rock and earth as Magnus climbed down into the hole with me.

"Are you sure?" he asked once he stood beside me.

"Positive. Look, you can even see pieces of collapsed support structures." I kept hauling rock aside until, eventually, I found exactly what I was looking for. Beneath the rubble lay the entrance to a tunnel leading deeper underground. It was perfectly square with clear support structures running along the walls.

"See," I said, pointing toward the tunnel that was just large enough for a person to walk through without hunching over. "This was manmade. That concrete slab that we assumed was an old building foundation must have been sealing off the entrance."

Now equally invested in our discovery, Magnus also inspected the support structures around the mouth of the tunnel. "Okay. But why? That concrete was old. It had obviously been here a long time. What's the point of building a tunnel like this if you're just going to seal it up?"

"I don't know," I said as I pulled a keychain from my belt that had a small flashlight attached. "But there's only one way to find out."

Pointing the light down the tunnel revealed that it was straight and mostly flat with only a slight downward slope. I took a few steps into the tunnel, careful not to hit my head on the ceiling. The tunnel had been built for an average sized man to pass through easily, but the original architects clearly hadn't anticipated someone of my size.

"Is it safe to go inside?" Magnus asked, even as he followed me. He was also forced to hunch, and his broad frame blocked most of the light coming in from the mouth of the tunnel until my small flashlight was the only thing illuminating the space.

"I wouldn't go much farther without proper supplies," I assured him, nodding down at my insufficient flashlight. "But these inner support structures seem stable. I'm not seeing any signs of damage or corrosion. The ones near the entrance must have been damaged when the cops dug up that coffin, but the rest of this is practically pristine. Whoever built this knew what they were doing."

The sound of shifting stone caught our attention. Magnus and I turned back toward the entrance of the tunnel, where Ellis and Trent had also climbed down into the hole and were now peering inside.

"Um, guys," Ellis said as he stared down into the dark, unable to see us in the shadows despite being only a few feet away. "I think you should come take a look at something."

Although only a difference of a few feet, the stark contrast of daylight compared to the darkness of the tunnel was blinding. I had to squint and wait for my eyes to readjust before I could see what Ellis and Trent had found.

Most of the broken support structures that lay scattered over the ground were in so many pieces they were barely recognizable, but a few sizable sections remained. One of the pieces, which Ellis and Trent were pointing at, still had its decorative carving.

Three familiar flowers formed a wreath carved directly into the rock.

I slapped Magnus upside the head. "How did you miss that?"

Scowling, Magnus brushed his ponytail back out of his face. "Hey. You missed it, too."

"Yeah, but you're the one who's obsessed with plants. Normally, they're the first thing you'd notice."

Magnus tried to punch my shoulder, but I dodged out of the way. "Well, excuse me for being distracted by the big fucking hole that just appeared in the middle of our home. I'm starting to wonder if these cults are right. The *Mothers of the Mountain* really are witches, and they've cursed this particular patch of land."

He said it as a joke, but there was something in his eyes, a raw emotion that begged me to prove his words were false.

"Witches aren't real, and this place ain't cursed," I assured him, turning my flashlight back to the dark tunnel. "There's just... a lot of mysteries."

Now that I knew what I was looking for, it was easier to find. Along the top of the tunnel, wreathes of roses, lisianthus, and poppy flowers had been carved right into the keystones of each support structure. It was clear who had built the tunnel, though I doubted the three sisters had constructed it themselves. They must have had help from their cult of followers. So many people working together to construct such a strong and elaborate tunnel, it must have led somewhere important.

The question now was, did it still lead anywhere?

Or had this tunnel been buried simply because it was no longer any use?

And why had they buried a body when they sealed it?

"Go get some more flashlights," I said as I stored my little keychain light back on my belt. "This isn't going to be enough."

Magnus was immediately onboard with the plan, and climbed out of the pit to go fetch flashlights from our houses. Ellis and Trent were more hesitant. They continued questioning me about whether the tunnel really was secure. Yet, in the end, their curiosity won out over their caution. When Magnus returned, they each took a flashlight from him.

The size of the tunnel meant we had to walk single file. I took the lead, with Magnus bringing up the rear, and Trent and Ellis in between us. Directly behind me, Ellis held his flashlight in one hand, swinging it around so quickly I doubted it was actually doing him much good. His other hand, which wasn't holding the flashlight, remained latched onto the bottom hem of my shirt.

Since meeting him, I'd gotten used to Ellis constantly clinging to me. The man was the calmest when he had a constant reminder of my presence. If he were anyone else, I would have found it smothering.

I surprised even myself when, instead of being annoyed, I merely found his clinginess endearing. The fact that Ellis found my presence so comforting brought a certain sense of pride that I could easily get addicted to. It was already clear that I was never going to push him away, and if I wasn't careful, I would probably just end up spoiling him and encouraging him to depend on me more.

In fact, that didn't sound like such a bad idea.

Just as I'd noticed before, the tunnel had a slight slope to it. While it looked straight at first, it was soon clear that we were heading farther underground. The air became cooler, and the shadows more oppressive. The flashlights we'd brought were of a decent quality, but even they could only do so much. The limited circles of light illuminated our path, but anywhere the flashlights weren't pointing was nothing but an empty void.

I walked with careful, deliberate steps, seeing the ground through my feet rather than my eyes.

Behind me, I could tell exactly where the others were simply by the sound of their footsteps.

Magnus walked with similar confidence as me. It wasn't the first time either of us had to explore unfamiliar territory while practically blind.

Ellis and Trent, however, were a different story. Trent's history as a competitive weightlifter meant he understood the importance of stable footing. His steps were solid, like the strike of a hammer hitting a nail squarely on the head, but it still took him an extra moment to find each step in the dark.

In contrast, Ellis's footsteps were all

over the place. Each step he took was hesitant and sounded as sturdy as a butterfly's wing. For such a large man, he made surprisingly little noise when he moved, like he was deliberately trying not to leave any evidence of his presence behind.

This was familiar territory, charging into an unknown situation with a team at my back. Yet, the addition of Ellis and Trent couldn't distract me from the fact that we were missing a set of footsteps.

Creed should have been here with us. He loved these kinds of unknown situations. Thrived on them. If he were here, he would have been leading the way while barking at the rest of us to hurry up.

I refused to entertain the idea that I would never hear his footsteps again. We'd received word that he was alive. Even if we didn't know the specifics of his situation or what was happening to him, I had to cling to the hope that he would be all right.

Anything else was unacceptable.

Distance was hard to judge in the cramped confines of the tunnel, but I estimated that we'd traveled about a hundred feet when the walls around us spread out. The tunnel abruptly widened, allowing us to walk two by two instead of single file, and I was even able to stand up straight.

It was a relief, and I rubbed the kink out of my neck from hunching over for so long as I studied what lay in front of us. The tunnel split into two paths, which explained the sudden change in size.

After seeing symbols of the same flowers so often, I was convinced that this time would be no different. So much so, that when I looked above the arch of one of the tunnels, I was legitimately surprised to see a simple circle and an X carved above the different doors.

"Ugh," Magnus groaned from the back of the group. "I know cults like being mysterious and everything, but just once couldn't they have labeled things with words instead of using symbols. How're we supposed to know what this means?"

"We're not," I said as I stepped under the archway marked with an X. "That's probably the point."

Ellis was still clinging to my shirt and had no choice but to come along with me as I inspected the tunnel I'd chosen.

Meanwhile, Magnus and Trent hung back in the tunnel's intersection.

"Um, we probably shouldn't go any farther," Trent said, the light from his flashlight disappearing for a moment as he checked the main tunnel we'd just come from. "Following a straight line is one thing, but if the tunnel keeps branching off then we're going to get lost. We need something to mark the path before we go any farther."

"I know," I called back and stopped just a few feet into the divergent tunnel. "I'm not going any farther. I just want to see if there's any indication about where these tunnels lead."

It was a fool's hope, but I couldn't turn back without making absolutely sure there wasn't some hint about what lay at the end of the tunnel.

There was nothing. Of course there wasn't. The stone and earth walls and the carefully built support structures of the tunnel were all the same. There was no indication of the purpose of the tunnel, but still I had to check.

Maybe, just this once, I shouldn't have been so thorough.

In the silence of the tunnel, a slight popping sound echoed as if it were a firecracker, followed shortly after by the shriek of sliding stone.

I pulled Ellis out of the way just as the entrance of the tunnel we stood in collapsed. Dirt and debris were thrown everywhere, making it nearly impossible to see even with the light of the flashlights, and the ground under our feet shook as large chunks of rock landed right where we'd been standing moments ago.

The chaos ended almost as quickly as it started, and Ellis and I were left standing there, staring at the pile of rock and earth where the entrance of the tunnel had once been.

"That shouldn't have happened," I said as I searched the nearby support structures that were still standing.

Ellis approached the pile of rubble blocking our path. "Well, clearly it did. Hey! Can you guys here us? Are you okay?"

On the other side of the collapsed rubble, Trent and Magnus's voices could just be heard shouting back at us.

I grabbed Ellis before he took another

step away from me.

"No. It shouldn't have collapsed."

Dread pooled in my stomach. There wasn't time for me to explain. All I could do was drag Ellis with me as I turned and ran the other direction down the tunnel.

Luckily, he didn't fight me and followed without complaint. Almost as soon as we started running, more of the tunnel collapsed.

One after another the support structures fell, their remnants piling on top of one another until the tunnel was packed tight with rock dirt.

I kept running until the noise of the collapsed ceased, and only when the tunnel fell silent again, did I dare stop.

Ellis leaned against me, panting heavily from our sudden sprint.

"What... the hell?" He gasped for breath, just as much from fear as from exhaustion. "I thought you said it was safe."

BRODY

"It was," I insisted, but Ellis wasn't listening.

"Clearly it wasn't. We never should have come down here."

"It was safe," I tried again, but Ellis was still too caught up in his terrified rant to hear me.

"Who even just goes down into a strange tunnel? Of course it was unstable. We only found it because it collapsed in the first place. We're idiots for coming down here."

"Ellis, listen to me." I grabbed his shoulder and shook him until I knew I had his attention. "It was safe. I know construction and building. I know the signs of an unsafe structure. It was safe. This tunnel shouldn't have just collapsed like that."

My mind returned to the slight popping sound I'd heard right before the collapse. That was not the sound of stone and wood breaking naturally.

"It shouldn't have collapsed," I repeated. "Not on its own."

Ellis took one look back at the pile of rubble only a few feet away, then his gaze returned to me and in his eyes was a new understanding.

"You think... someone made it collapse?"

"I think you should stay very, very close to me."

Letting him go, I reached under my jacket and pulled out a handgun from the holster clipped to my belt. With the gun in one hand and my flashlight in the other, I pointed both down the open end of the tunnel.

"You're armed?" Ellis gasped out, while practically plastering himself to my back.

"I'm always armed."

"Of course you are," he sighed. "Why am I even surprised?"

My flashlight didn't penetrate the darkness very far, and even with Ellis adding his own light into the mix, the open tunnel still stood before us like a solid black curtain.

I started moving down the tunnel, pushing forward into the black, but before I could take more than two steps, Ellis clung to me so tightly I was trapped in place.

"Shouldn't we stay here?" he asked, speaking directly into my ear. "If we leave, Magnus and Trent won't be able to find us."

My gaze never left the open maw of the tunnel stretching before us, even as I answered him. "There's dozens of yards of debris between us and them, now. It would take an entire excavation team for them to reach us. No. Our best bet is to keep going."

"But—" he started to argue, but I cut him off.

"Listen. Whoever built these tunnels knew what they were doing. They would have built other exits just in case one was cut off. There must be another way out farther down the tunnel, so we need to keep going. Besides, I don't want to wait around here for whoever sabotaged the tunnel to bring the rest of the structure down on our heads."

Although I couldn't see him, I could feel Ellis's whole body shaking as he pressed himself against my back. I couldn't let go of my gun or my flashlight to reach out to him, but with him so close, it was easy to simply turn my head a bit and press my lips to his cheek.

"Trust me?"

He swallowed hard enough that I could hear his throat moving. Then he stopped shaking and nodded.

"Yeah. Yeah, I trust you."

"All right. Then come on, stay close, and do exactly as I tell you."

Ellis barely allowed an inch of air between our bodies. As we pressed forward into the darkness, we moved as one unit, so in sync that the echoes of our footsteps were indistinguishable from each other.

CHAPTER TWELVE

Ellis

WE SEEMED TO walk forever. Down in the darkness of the tunnel, it felt like time wasn't moving at all. Our phones didn't work so far underground, and only Brody's wristwatch let us track the passing hours.

Nothing in the tunnel changed. No matter how far we traveled, the tunnel just kept stretching forward in a straight, never-ending line. As evening rolled around, unseen above our heads, my strength began to wane. We had neither food nor water, and although we weren't traveling quickly, the endless walking still took a toll on me.

I didn't say a word about my exhaustion and was determined to keep going, even as I dragged my feet. We must have covered miles without an end in sight, and Brody didn't look tired at all. The man probably could have carried on at the same steady pace all night, and I refused to drag him down.

I would just have to find a way to keep up.

Another hour passed, and night must have settled in properly by then. Each step felt a little harder than the last, and I clung to the back of Brody's shirt like it was a lifeline.

The man never faltered. He'd hardly lowered his gun all day.

Didn't his arms hurt?

I knew he was strong, but this seemed

ridiculous.

I suddenly tripped over some loose stones on the floor and fell against Brody's back. My weight would have flattened a weaker man, but Brody barely flinched. He stopped in the middle of the tunnel and lowered his gun for the first time that day to wrap an arm around me.

"Sorry. We should have taken a break sooner. You must be exhausted. Here. Sit down."

He tried to lead me over to a spot where I could sit and lean against the wall, but I refused.

"No, its fine," I insisted. "I can keep going."

Grabbing onto my arm, Brody forcefully dragged me over to the wall. "Ellis. You've been walking all day without any breaks. You need to rest."

"So have you."

"Well, I should rest, too."

To prove his point, Brody sat down on

the side of the tunnel, leaned against the wall, and patted the floor beside him in invitation.

I would have kept arguing, but I really was tired. So, with a huff, I sat down beside him and automatically leaned against his shoulder.

We turned off our flashlights to preserve the batteries, relying only on Brody's little keychain light to see. The weak little glow barely let me see his face, but even that was enough to show that Brody was still on guard. His eyes never stopped scanning the darkness around us, and his gun remained firmly in his hand and at the ready.

"I don't know how you do it," I mumbled as my eyelids drifted closed without my permission. "All I've been doing is following you, and I'm tired. How do you still have the energy to say alert?"

Beside me, Brody shifted for a moment before I felt his lips pressed against my forehead.

"Practice," he said, his breath ruffling my bangs. "I spent years training for these kinds of situations. So don't feel bad. Okay? Rest when you need to rest. I'll be right here."

I mumbled something that was meant to be a protest, but exhaustion slurred my words into a garbled mess. Before I knew it, I drifted off to sleep using his shoulder as a pillow.

***

When I woke up, it was so dark that I couldn't immediately tell if my eyes were open or not. It seemed like no time at all had passed since I fell asleep, but the grogginess that clouded my brain and clung to the corners of my consciousness said that I'd probably slept for a while.

"Brody?" I said, barely managing to get my lips around that single word. Every part of my body ached, and moving even a single muscle took a ridiculous amount of effort.

That's what I got for falling asleep sitting up at my age. I should have known better. Sleeping against a wall wasn't even comfortable when I was twenty. At the age of forty-five, I'd probably be feeling the effects of the stone against my back for weeks.

"Ellis," Brody's deep voice greeted me from the dark. "I'm here."

Something shifted under my head, reminding me that I was lying on his shoulder, and he turned his keychain light on so I could see him.

After getting used to the dark of the cave, even that small glow felt too bright, and I had to squint.

Brody was in almost the exact same position as he'd been when I fell asleep. The only difference was that he'd raised one knee to casually support his hand that was holding the gun. He would have seemed relaxed, if not for the stiff set to his shoulders and the sharp look in his eyes.

"Have you been sitting here in the dark this whole time?" I asked. There was no point in asking if he'd guarded me the whole time I slept. That answer was obvious.

Brody just shrugged, moving one shoulder more than the other to avoid jostling me. "No point in having the light on when we're not moving. This tunnel is so quiet, I'd hear anyone approaching long before I could see them, even with the light on."

That may be true, but I couldn't imagine keeping my cool while staring off into the dark for hours, just waiting for the slightest sound of danger. My nerves would probably be shredded after just half an hour.

"How long has it been?" I asked as I sat up.

Brody checked his watch.

"A few hours. It's the middle of the night right now. You can sleep a little more, if you want."

"No. We should keep going. The sooner we get moving, the sooner we get out of here."

Despite the pain in my joints and the ache in my back, sleeping had at least refreshed my energy. I kept up with Brody much more easily as we continued our journey down the tunnel, thankfully, with both of our flashlights turned on.

More hours passed, and I no longer bothered to ask about the time. I didn't want to know if morning had rolled around or if it was still night outside. The thought of spending an entire day trapped down in this tunnel was too depressing to contemplate, and I preferred to ignore it.

I was so focused on the little circle of light made by my flashlight, and my efforts not to trip over my own feet in the dark, that I didn't notice that Brody had stopped walking until I ran right into him. Luckily, he seemed to expect it and used the arm holding his own flashlight to brace me.

"Hold on," he said, pointing his flashlight forward once again. "There's something up ahead."

It was faint at first, but as we cautiously crept closer, I could eventually see that the tunnel opened into a larger space. At first, I feared we'd come to another split in the tunnel, like the one that had separated us from Magnus and Trent.

Instead, what we found was a single, large door. An opening in the ceiling above let in a thin stream of sunlight, letting me know that night had passed, and it was now the next day. Based on the height of the ceiling, and how weak the sunlight was, we were much farther underground than I wanted to think about.

To distract myself from the weight of the earth and stone above our heads, I focused on the door in front of us, precisely illuminated by the ray of sunlight. It was the size of a bank vault, covered in intricate carvings of flowers and vines all around. There was no obvious handle or way through the door. Not even a keyhole that would let us peer through to the other side.

"This is a door, right?" I asked, approaching the door when Brody didn't stop me. "I don't see any way in."

The carvings on the door were even more intricate than I first thought. I could feel individual veins on the stone leaves, and every petal on every flower was unique. I didn't know much about flowers, but even I could pick out the three distinct types woven together as they climbed up the surface of the door.

Brody also inspected the door, but

rather than use his eyes, he leaned his ear against the stone and tapped at it with the handle of his flashlight. I couldn't hear any difference as he tapped at different spots, but Brody must have picked up something, because his tapping led him to a spot in the middle of the door, just below waist height.

One of the carved leaves, which looked no different than any other spot on the design, slid aside to reveal a keyhole.

I stepped up beside Brody, staring at this small anomaly in the otherwise seamless door. "Can you open it?"

It wouldn't surprise me if lockpicking was also one of his skills. The man was the human equivalent of a Swiss army knife. Every time I thought I found the extent of his abilities; he pulled out something new.

"Maybe," Brody hummed as he examined the keyhole, giving credence to my thought that he really could pick the lock if he wanted. "Although, we may not have to. The leaf this keyhole was hidden under specifically belongs to the poppy plant on this design. Everything else the *Mothers of the Mountain* made has been so specific with their details. The fact that the keyhole was hidden under a poppy leaf must mean the door belongs to Poppy Milford."

Letting the leaf swing back into place and cover the hole, Brody turned to me with an expectant look.

"Do you still have that key your brother gave you?"

Ever since the discovery of this tunnel, I hadn't even thought about the key that sat in my pocket. Now, it suddenly felt as though it weighed ten pounds, and I could swear the metal grew warm under my hand when I pulled it out.

The key that had been my brother's last act of defiance in his life.

The key that I'd nearly lost my life in

order to keep hidden.

The key that was engraved with poppy flowers.

Silently, with trembling fingers, I handed the key to Brody.

"You do it. I don't... I don't think I can."

Brody just nodded and turned back to the door. He didn't demand any further explanation. He didn't need one. He already understood how many different emotions I had tied up in that key.

As Brody lined the key up with the keyhole, I took a step back to give him and the door space. It was the first time since entering the tunnel that I'd been more than an arm's length away from him.

Surely, I thought, nothing bad could happen in the time it took to unlock a door.

I was wrong.

That one brief moment of distance

between us was my downfall.

A sharp yank on my hair snapped my head backwards while at the same time my feet were kicked out from under me. I fell, landing hard on the floor and smashing my knee down hard on the stone as I struggled to keep myself upright.

The grip on my hair forced my head back farther, and something hard and cold pressed against the underside of my jaw.

I'd become familiar with what the barrel of a gun felt like, unfortunately.

The key dropped to the ground as Brody pointed his own weapon and the unknown person standing behind me.

"Let him go."

My captor's gun dug harder into my skin.

"You know I can't do that," the man holding me hostage said with a voice that would have been pleasant if it wasn't filled with such malice. "But I can promise not to hurt him if you hand that key over now."

With my head yanked back, I could only see Brody out of the corner of my eye. I couldn't see the expression on his face, but I could feel the tension filling the stale air of the tunnel as Brody kicked Poppy's key over toward my captor.

More people stepped into view from behind my back, weapons trained on Brody as one of them picked up the key.

How many people were there?

I could almost understand one person sneaking up on us while Brody was distracted with the door, but so many?

It didn't make sense.

Pulling against the grip on my hair, I managed to snatch a look behind me. There was a small doorway off to the side that definitely hadn't been there before. It must have been hidden or disguised to look like just another part of the wall.

Even I wasn't careless enough to overlook an entire door.

The hand in my hair pulled harder, forcing me to look forward again.

"Eyes up front," my captor ordered.

I hissed at the stab of pain. This was nothing like when Brody pulled my hair in bed. That pain was soft. It blended with pleasure, and most importantly, it was wanted. This wasn't wanted, which instantly made it a thousand times worse.

Gritting my teeth together, I looked up into my captor's eyes. "So, which cult are you with? You obviously know these tunnels, so you might belong to the *Mothers of the Mountain*. But you were willing to sabotage the tunnels, so you might belong to *The Tamed Souls*. Which one is it?"

The man holding me captive was disappointingly ordinary. He was the kind of person I wouldn't have looked at twice if I passed him on the street. Even now, I wouldn't have found him very noteworthy, even as he shook my head so hard I feared it would snap right off my neck.

"Don't you dare lump us in with those sanctimonious little whores."

"Right," I said while desperately trying not to bite off my own tongue. "So, *The Tamed Souls,* then. I should have guessed. You seem to have a fetish for taking me hostage."

Brody took another step closer, and every gun except the one digging into my chin aimed right between his eyes.

"Let. Him. Go."

Even without seeing Brody's expression, I could feel the heat of fury radiating from him with every word he spoke.

My captor merely laughed. "No need to get so angry. If you need to blame anyone, then blame his traitor of a brother. We wouldn't have needed to resort to such measures if that bastard hadn't stolen from us.”

I grabbed onto the man's wrist to try and keep him from pulling out any more of my hair as I glared up at him.

"He only stole from you because you lied to him. You said you could save him and instead, you took advantage of a dying man."

My captor didn't even have the decency to look guilty at the accusation.

"Our order is only interested in saving souls. The mortal body is of no concern of ours. If your brother misinterpreted our gospel, that's his own fault. Not ours. Now, tell your friend there to hand over his gun, or your soul will soon be joining your brother in damnation."

No way in hell was I going to tell Brody to hand over his gun. I may not be able to fight, some days I could barely even take care of myself, but I wasn't so useless that I would endanger the man I cared about to save my own life.

BRODY

It didn't matter, anyway. Brody took the hint without me even needing to ask. He dropped his gun to the ground and kicked it over toward my captors the same as he had done with the key.

"Very good," my captor said with a mocking tone as one of his accomplices also snatched up Brody's gun. "Now, let's get going. I'm not going to stand around in this tunnel all day."

Brody was ushered off to the side of the tunnel, as far from me as the space would allow and always with several guns pointed at him. My own captor, meanwhile, barely seemed to notice that he had a gun pointed at my head.

It was obvious which of the two of us they considered more dangerous.

Using Poppy Milford's key, our captors unlocked the large door. It had no handle, but as soon as the lock clicked into place, several of the carved vines moved as if they were growing up the door right before our eyes. The door swung open on its own, eerily silent on its old hinges.

The outside of the door was the size of a vault, but on the inside, it was as large as a cavern. Stairs were carved directly into the stone, leading to the floor, which was at least a full story below the door. Most of the rock had been left in its natural state, but there were a few carvings here and there to show that the cavern had been constructed with intent. All three of the Milford sisters' namesake flowers were present in the carvings, but there was a definite emphasis on the poppy flower overall. While all three sisters must have had a hand in this secret underground vault, it was clear who was responsible for it overall.

The stairs were narrow, so our group could only descend one at a time. I went down first, with my captor right behind me, keeping his gun trained directly between my shoulder blades. Only once I was brought to the bottom of the stairs and to the other side of the cavern was Brody then escorted down under armed guard.

"Kind of excessive, don't you think?"

My captor just scoffed.

"I've seen that man's military record. Trust me. Nothing is too excessive."

"Trust you? Yeah, sure. I'll get right on it."

I spoke with as much sarcasm as I could muster to hide the fact that his words had hit a bit too close to home. In all the time I'd known him, Brody had made some vague comments about his time in the military, but never told me anything concrete. No horrific war stories, or funny anecdotes from his training days. It was as if, the moment he retired, that part of his life was locked away behind a sealed door even more impressive than the one leading into this cavern. I hated that there was such an important part of him that I didn't know, almost as much as I hated the fact that the man holding me hostage seemed to know more about Brody's past than I did.

"If he's so dangerous, then why risk taking us captive. Surely, you could have figured out a way down here without us."

I had meant for my comment to point out how stupid it was for them to take us captive in the first place. However, as soon as the words left my mouth, I realized my mistake. My comment could just as easily serve as a reminder that, now that they had the key, there was no reason to keep us alive anymore.

Pressed almost intimately against my back, with his hand fisted in my hair, my captor laughed in my ear and pressed his gun harder against me. "I could kill you both right now. It would certainly save us some trouble. However, you might still be of use retrieving Angus Grieve's body."

Angus Grieve? I'd never heard the

name before.

Momentarily forgetting about the gun pressed against me, I turned to look at my captor over my shoulder.

"Grieve? Who the hell is that?"

Without warning, my captor suddenly reared his hand back and slapped me hard across the face. My whole world spun, and I fell to the ground like a puppet whose puppeteer had suddenly abandoned him. In the distance, I heard Brody calling my name, but it was drowned out by my captor's furious shouting.

"Don't you dare play dumb with me. After over a century of searching, our founder's body was finally located, only for the police to lock it away as evidence and keep it from us. You and these other damned sodomites have been hindering us at every turn, so you are going to shut up and finally make yourselves useful for a higher cause."

I was still too dizzy after the sudden blow to get up, so I didn't even try. I simply lay on the ground and waited for the cavern to stop spinning, muttering under my breath about how many head injuries one person could withstand in a short amount of time. Surely, I was reaching the limit by now.

At least we'd finally identified the body that Magnus and Brody had found. If my captor was to be believed, the corpse's name was Angus Grieve, and he was the founder of *The Tamed Souls*. How he ended up buried in a concrete foundation was still unknown, but at least we'd solved one part of the mystery.

Sometime while I was regaining my senses on the floor, my captor and his cronies continued with their plans. Brody was subdued and tied up in a far corner—still kept under the watch of an armed guard—while my captor located the vault's contents.

BRODY

It wasn't hard to find.

A single stone podium stood at the center of the cavern, about chest height and only two feet across. A small wooden box sat on top of the podium, clearly very important despite its stark simplicity.

That was it. The cavern held nothing else. This entire vault had been built down beneath the surface of the earth just to hide whatever was inside that box.

Another of *The Tamed Souls* members grabbed me by my hair and forced me to my feet. A new gun was pointed at me, and I was once against left in the exact same position as before, but my captor was now free to approach the podium at the center of the room.

His hands shook as he picked up the box, tracing his fingers around the simple edges as if savoring the moment before he opened it.

What could be so important?

A few days ago, Deputy Hillard had

told us a story about how the Mothers of the Mountain had actually been born into *The Tamed Souls* cult, but eventually escaped and founded their own cult within Emberwood. Supposedly, as they fled, they'd stolen something from the leader of *The Tamed Souls* cult. It was unknown what exactly they'd stolen, but it must have been something important for them to bother going to the trouble.

Could the stolen item be inside that box?

It seemed so small, but the value of an object wasn't always equivalent to its size.

My captor slowly opened the box.

In the dim light of the cavern, I watched as the elated expression on the man's face melted away into confusion, and then shock.

"What?" Several other cult members called out as they crowded around the box. "What is it?"

Letting the box fall from his hands so

it hit the ground with a loud crash, my captor held up the object that had been contained within.

It was a single wooden dowel, cylindrical in shape and about eight inches long. It had been polished, so the dowel had been made intentionally, but otherwise, it looked no different than a piece of scrap wood you could find at any hardware store.

One of the other cult members snatched the dowel from my captor's hands, turning it over as if the dowel's true meaning might be carved on the underside of the wood. "Is this some sort of joke? This can't be it."

It sounded like even these cult members didn't know what the *Mothers of the Mountain* had stolen from their founder, but they'd obviously expected something much more impressive.

I didn't dare to do so out loud, but internally I laughed at their plight.

"No," the cult member shouted as he threw the dowel to the ground. "They're making fools of us. We've come all this way just for a damn wild goose chase."

My captor retrieved the dowel, still handling it as though it were a precious object. "It can't be a trick. We know those sisters stole something from our founder. Something so important he went after them to retrieve it. They killed him to keep him from getting it back and hid his body where it wouldn't be found for generations. Why go through all of that, why build this whole vault then hide the key and the entrance, if it was just a trick. It doesn't make sense."

The cult members were growing angrier by the second. They'd come here expecting riches or ancient secrets and were instead, left with trash. In the heat of their disappointment, they quickly turned on each other. One cult member knocked the dowel from my captor's hands, while another pointed their weapon at him.

"Do you have any idea how many risks we've taken all because you promised us that it would be worth it in the end," the cult member pointing the gun shouted. "We've broken the law. We've stolen. We've taken hostages. Now there's a target on our back, and for what? We all know these military men are dangerous. They may be retired, but we've seen firsthand what they're capable of, and now we've made an enemy out of them for nothing. We'd have been better off never getting involved."

The hand in my hair relaxed slightly as the cult member holding me captive was distracted by the growing argument.

I might have been able to get away from him, but what good would it do?

They were still armed when I wasn't, and Brody was tied up on the other side of the cavern. Even if I managed to free myself, I'd be gunned down before I could do anything.

Rather than be intimidated by his own people waving a gun in his face, my captor only grew bolder. Standing up straight to his full height, he stared his fellow cult member down and smacked the end of the gun away from him.

"You think these military bastards are too dangerous? Fine. Let's take care of it." Taking hold of the same gun that he had previously pressed under my chin, he cocked back the hammer with an echoing click of metal. "Doesn't matter how dangerous they are. They're not a threat once they're dead."

With his gun primed, he turned toward Brody.

A voice screamed inside my head, but no sound came from my mouth. I was frozen in shock as I watched my captor advance on Brody, gun ready to fire at any moment. Brody struggled against his restraints, blue-green eyes blazing with hate at the approaching danger, but he couldn't get himself free.

"No," I screamed in my mind. "Not again. I'd already buried one person I loved. I couldn't do it again."

I didn't even think about acting. I just moved. I slammed my head backward into the face of the cult member standing behind me. His nose broke against the strength of my skull, and he staggered backward. I didn't even notice the pain from the impact as I spun and grabbed his gun from his hand.

I knew nothing about weapons. I couldn't even identify what type of gun I held. However, I didn't need any special training to understand the most basic concept of a gun.

Aim the barrel and pull the trigger.

So, I did.

The shot echoed like a bomb in the cavern. Everyone jumped in surprise, including me. The kickback from the shot was stronger than I expected, straining my wrist and sending the gun flying right out of my hand.

For a moment everyone froze. I was certain that I had missed. I'd barely even aimed the gun, just pointed in the general direction I wanted the bullet to go.

However, after a moment of stunned silence, my captor dropped to his knees only a few feet away from Brody, his hand pressed against his stomach. Blood immediately seeped between his fingers.

Chaos erupted.

The other cult members ran for their injured companion, trying to patch up his wound.

I should have been doing something. I should have taken advantage of the distraction to get to Brody, but all I could do was stand there in stunned shock.

I'd actually hit him. For the first time in my life, I'd fought back, and it had worked. Minutes ago, that man had held my life in his hands, and now, he was on the ground bleeding from a hole in his stomach that I'd put there.

It was terrifying.

A hand grabbed my arm. At first, I instinctively pulled away, until I realized it was Brody. He'd done what I failed to do and used the distraction as an opportunity to escape. His hands were still bound together, but his feet were free and that was all he needed.

"Come on," he said as he dragged me toward the vault door. "Let's get out of here."

At that same moment the cult members noticed our escape, but it was too late. Brody and I were already up the stairs and out the door. Without the key, we couldn't close it behind us. The hidden door that the cult members had used to sneak up on us was still open. So, we headed down that smaller tunnel, hand in hand off into the dark as we ran for our lives.

CHAPTER THIRTEEN

Brody

WE HAD NO idea where we were going as we ran off into the pitch black. The tunnel behind the hidden door that our attackers had used to sneak up on us could lead anywhere.

But anywhere had to be better than where we'd just escaped.

That had been far too close. I knew something was suspicious when the tunnel collapsed and cut us off from Magnus and Trent. The supports had been stable and shouldn't have caved in so suddenly. It was clear someone was trying to set a trap for us, yet I'd still allowed them to sneak up on us.

I hadn't been retired from the military that long. Just less than a year. Yet, my skills were already getting rusty if a bunch of barely trained civilians could get the drop on me.

My fingers were going numb from the strength of Ellis's grip on my hand as we ran blindly through the dark.

I should have been paying attention to where we were going. The tunnel wasn't completely black now. Some light managed to leak through cracks in the ceiling, meaning we weren't too far underground. However, all I could think about was my worry for Ellis. The man hadn't said anything, but I knew he had to be panicking. He'd just shot a man. It had been a gut shot, not immediately fatal, but there was a very real possibility that he'd just taken a life.

I remembered my first kill. It had been in the middle of battle. I was posted up on a high perspective to offer cover fire for the rest of the unit. There had been more enemies than we predicted, and my commanding officer's voice had come through the radio piece in my ear, ordering me to take the shot. I'd acted automatically, just like I always had in practice, but the moment after I pulled the trigger and watched a man's body collapse through the scope on my gun, I felt my whole world shift around me. I'd crossed a line I could never come back from, and even though I'd known it was coming, I still wasn't prepared. Nothing could truly prepare you for taking a life.

I struggled with myself for a while afterward, trying to come to terms with my new identity as a murderer.

Sanctioned murder, but still murder.

Right now, Ellis was probably still in

fight or flight mode, so he hadn't processed the fact that he'd shot a man, but it was bound to catch up with him eventually.

I didn't want that. Ellis deserved to live his life in innocence, without the weight of another man's life on his conscience.

If only I could have been the one to pull the trigger instead. I'd chosen my path, and the weight of one more life would be nothing compared to the burdens I already carried.

"I think there's something up ahead," Ellis said as we ran, snapping me out of my thoughts.

Sure enough, the light leaking through the ceiling revealed that the tunnel dead-ended into a staircase that led to the surface. The two of us paused at the bottom of the stairs. They weren't that tall. Maybe only about twenty feet. It was close enough for us to see that the stairs lead to a large rectangular trapdoor in the ceiling.

Ellis looked at me for direction. "Do we go up? I mean, we have to, right? There's nowhere else for us to go."

He was right, of course. There was no other path for us, but before I could say as much, the decision was made for us. Voices sounded in the tunnel, approaching from behind. The cult members had followed us, and by the sound of it they were gaining quickly.

There was no time for second-guessing. Holding tight to Ellis's hand, I pulled him up the stairs with me.

The trapdoor had a complicated latch. For a moment, I feared we were trapped, but the latch turned easily under my hand. Sounds of grinding stone and moving gears echoed through the tunnel as the trap door opened. It split down the middle and slid aside like a pair of elevator doors, blinding us with the sudden glow of daylight.

The trap door led into the bottom of a large stone box. Luckily, it was only a couple feet tall, so climbing out wasn't a problem, but Ellis's foot snagged on the edge of the stone as he stepped over and sent us both crashing to the ground.

I kept Ellis close, letting my body take the brunt of the fall. The force of the impact knocked the air from my lungs. When I shook off the blow enough to look up, I found a pair of sturdy black boots standing right in front of me.

"What the hell have you gotten yourself into?" someone demanded.

I knew that voice.

Looking up so quickly I nearly snapped my own neck, I called out in surprise.

"Creed!"

It had been months since I'd last seen the man through anything other than a screen, but he looked exactly the same. Same dark hair, same stern face, and the same intimidating build, as if he could block out the sun with the width of his shoulders alone.

And, at the moment, there was a very familiar scowl on his face.

"I leave you idiots alone for a few months and you're getting chased around by murderous cults. I shouldn't have even bothered coming. You and Magnus deserve to get shot."

My joy at seeing my old friend was momentarily pushed to the back of my mind as I remembered our current situation. Looking around, I realized we were back in the Milford sisters' hidden mausoleum, and Ellis and I had just crawled out of Poppy Milford's tomb.

"What are you doing here?" I asked Creed, not sure if I was demanding to know how he'd found the hidden mausoleum, or what he was doing stateside at all.

Last I'd heard, he'd been captured by the enemy somewhere overseas and had possibly been rescued. Now, suddenly, here he was right in front of me, on the other side of the globe from where he was supposed to be.

Before Creed could answer, voices floated up from the opening to the staircase inside Poppy Milford's grave. The cult members were still following us.

Creed held out a hand, palm facing toward me.

"Wait here. I'll take care of it."

Just before he disappeared into the darkness of the underground tunnel, I saw him pull out a gun from his belt and knew how he planned to "take care" of things.

Ellis latched onto my arm, plastering himself to my side. "Brody, who... What's going on?"

He was shaking from head to toe, and for the first time since we started running, I realized he still held the gun he'd used to save me.

"Hey, Ellis. It's okay. I can take that now."

The metal of the gun practically rattled in his hand, and it was a miracle he hadn't accidentally pulled the trigger by now. I had to help him pry his fingers off of the handle, and then shoved it into the empty holster on my own belt for safekeeping.

Down inside the tunnel, people started shouting, and a gunshot rang through the air.

"Come on," I said as I led Ellis away from the open tomb. "Let's get out of here."

Outside the tunnel, we were immediately greeted by Deputy Hillard, who came running up to us with several officers in tow.

"That man, Creed Landry, where'd he go?"

Still shocked from the sudden turn of events, I just pointed back inside the mausoleum.

Deputy Hillard sighed and hurried his people into the mausoleum. "I told him to wait for us. This is a police matter. We need to be the ones to handle it."

I could have told Deputy Hillard that his orders were pointless. Creed would never stay behind while people he cared about were in danger. Even our commanding officers had trouble keeping control of him, and he probably would have been dishonorably discharged long ago if he wasn't so good at his job.

However, Deputy Hillard and the other law enforcement officers were already charging into the mausoleum before I could say a word, and didn't bother shouting after him. He could learn for himself how impossible Creed could be.

A blanket fell over my shoulders. I whirled around, newly acquired gun halfway out of its holster before I realized who stood beside me.

BRODY

"Damn it, Mag," I shouted, shoving the gun back into its holster. "Don't sneak up on me. I nearly shot you."

Beside me, Magnus eyed my hand, which was still on my gun, but he didn't look worried.

"You? The expert sniper? Nah. You've got too much control for that."

"Not right now, I don't."

Off to the side, I noticed Trent holding out another blanket for Ellis. It seemed like everyone was suddenly showing up out of the woodwork. The once secret mausoleum was turning into a regular hangout spot.

Still, with the arrival of other people I trusted, I was finally able to let my guard down. I practically collapsed onto a nearby log and hung my head in my hands, letting out a long groan as the tension in my shoulders released.

"This last day has been hell, Mag."

Ellis sat quietly beside me, barely

moving the log. If it wasn't for the way he pressed up against my side, I may not have even realized he was there.

Magnus, in contrast, was impossible to ignore as he roughly slapped my shoulder.

"Tell me about it. When you two disappeared behind that cave-in, I thought for sure you were dead. I ran into town to get help, and Creed just suddenly showed up." Sighing heavily, he ran a hand through his already disheveled hair, pulling free what little remained in his blond braid. "I thought I was dreaming when he just appeared out of nowhere. What is he even doing here?"

"I was hoping you'd tell me," I said, shaking my own head. More gunfire could be heard coming from inside the mausoleum, faint but unmistakable. "We'll have to ask him about it later, but for now, I'm just glad he's here."

"Yeah," Magnus agreed as he took a

seat on a nearby stump. "Oh, by the way. here. I figured you'd probably need this."

He and Trent handed over a few water bottles, granola bars, and some jerky. It wasn't much, but after not eating anything for over a day while hiking miles underground and then fighting for our lives, Ellis and I were both starving. Even such basic food tasted like a five-star buffet.

With my stomach no longer growling at me, I immediately felt much better. I put an arm around Ellis, intending to comfort him, but there wasn't really anything to say. The situation was what it was. No amount of words were going to change things.

All four of us ended up sitting there in silence, listening to the noises of the forest as we waited to see what would happen.

It took nearly an hour, but eventually, Creed reemerged with a few of Deputy

Hillard's officers in tow. They brought with them some of the cult members that had attacked us, tied up in handcuffs and dumped face first onto the forest floor.

Only half the cult members that attacked us were present. I didn't question what happened to the others. Whenever Creed pulled out a gun, he never left his enemies alive.

Surprisingly, the man that Ellis had shot was still alive. A hasty bandage had been wrapped around his stomach, which at this point was more red than white. He was unconscious due to the blood loss, but was clearly still breathing.

"Hopefully, we'll be able to get some information out of these fuckers," Creed said as he dumped the last captured man into the ground. "Although, I'm regretting keeping so many alive. It's going to be a bitch getting all six of them out of the forest while they're handcuffed."

The man that Ellis had shot groaned

into the dirt, and Creed nudged him with his foot. "Well, depending how long it takes, maybe only five."

If we were out on the battlefield, I would have agreed with Creed. Lugging a prisoner who was already on death's door through the forest wasn't worth the effort when time could soon solve the problem for us. However, when I looked over at Ellis, I noticed the ashen tint to his face as he stared at the man he had shot. Ellis wouldn't speak up. He'd let the man bleed out if I said it was the best option, but it would also haunt him.

Ellis had already been through enough. He didn't need this burden as well.

"Six," I said with a tone of finality. "We're taking all six of them back. Alive."

At first Creed looked at me with confusion, but quickly got the message when I glanced pointedly over at Ellis.

"Right. We're taking all six back. Guess

I better bandage this guy up a bit better so he can actually get to a hospital."

As Creed went to fetch more medical supplies from the officers, I watched as the tension melted away from Ellis. After so many years of military training, I hated leaving an enemy alive unnecessarily. It was just one more danger that could come back to bite us in the future. Yet, I didn't regret it.

Whatever threat we may face later was worth the peace that I was able to bring Ellis now.

***

Deputy Hillard and the other law enforcement officers took their time clearing out the underground tunnels, making sure that no other members of *The Tamed Souls* had slipped their notice. They didn't find anyone else lurking around, but they did find something interesting that they said we should see.

BRODY

All five of us—Creed, Magnus, Trent, Ellis, and myself—were brought back down underground into a tunnel we hadn't seen before. Apparently, there was a whole system of them branching out from the mausoleum that led to various points around the forest, and even a few that seemed to lead in town. The place they wanted us to see wasn't too far away, and after only a few minutes of walking, we found ourselves in a large area that had clearly been dug out a long time ago.

"It's a mine?" I asked as I looked around.

"Yeah," Deputy Hillard said as he ran his hands over parts of the wall that still bore rough tool marks. "There seems to be veins of both silver and gold here. A significant portion of it has already been mined out, but there is still a ton left. It could even stretch all the way through the mountain."

Without knowing where the tunnels of

the mine led, we didn't dare venture too far and mostly stayed close to the main cavern where most of the tunnels branched out from. About two stories tall, it was an impressive size. It had obviously taken many workers to construct, but there was something familiar about the overall design. When trapped in a narrow tunnel with only a flashlight to see by, I hadn't noticed it before, but now that I was able to get a good look at so much of the design at once, I recognized the style.

"Poppy Milford designed the mine. She probably even had a hand in building it herself."

The mine was in good condition, but still old. There was loose rubble over the floor, and areas where the ground had clearly been disturbed. Magnus nearly tripped over his own feet as he attempted to look at the ceiling and watch the floor at the same time. His interests lay in the living things that could be grown from the earth, not in the raw materials that could be harvested from under the soil, so he only gave the mine a cursory glance. However, at the mention of Poppy Milford's name, his interest was piqued, and he turned to me with a new spark in his eye.

"How can you tell? I'm sure the sisters were involved since these tunnels connect to their own mausoleum, but how can you tell that they actually built it?"

I ran a hand over one of the nearby support structures, taking note of the way the materials had been manipulated and the overall grace of the design.

"Any builder with enough experience will develop a style. For example, anyone with a keen eye for construction will be able to tell that I built both of our houses, based on the way that I choose to put things together. The mine, the tunnels, the vault, everything down here was built by the same person."

Magnus looked around again, as if he expected to see evidence of what I was talking about, but unsurprisingly there was no more recognition in his eyes than there had been before.

"Okay? But how do you know it was Poppy Milford? Just because the vault had more Poppies on it than other flowers? Someone could have just designed it for her."

"Perhaps, but the same person also created Rose's locket, and those archways you found leading to the mausoleum from the old mill. It was all made by the same hand." I tapped a spot on one of the support structures, where metal had been welded together in a circular pattern that resembled a flower. "Besides, this craftsman likes to sign their work. There're poppy flowers hidden all over the place if you know where to look."

"It doesn't matter who built it," Creed interrupted us. "More importantly, this mine explains how these sisters had so much influence in the town and formed their own cult in the first place. The resources here would have been worth a fortune, and money talks. They couldn't easily have bought people's favor."

Having Creed back after months of being apart was so odd, yet so comfortable at the same time. It was like suddenly having an arm reattached that I didn't know was missing in the first place. He easily slipped right back into his position as the third member of our trio, and for a moment, I almost felt like I was back on the frontlines.

In order to see down in the mine, several large spotlights had been set up. They cast strange shadows in every direction and accentuated the harsh look on Deputy Hillard's face when he approached us.

"The *Mothers of the Mountain* didn't have to buy anyone. Their abilities allowed them to find this mine when the town needed finances after the fire. The profits saved this town."

Creed kept himself partially concealed in the shadows so his expression was hidden, but I could tell from his posture that he wasn't amused.

"So, you're saying that the Milford sisters... what? Were able to magically locate the mine when they needed it?"

Since he couldn't see Creed's expression, and didn't know how to read the other man's body language, Deputy Hillard made the mistake of thinking Creed's question was genuine.

"Exactly," he said, looking happy that he was believed. "That's why they are called the *Mothers of the Mountain.* Because they were brought here to take care of the land."

I pulled Creed away before he could argue further, shuffling him toward Magnus, where the two of us could, hopefully, keep him in check. I'd missed Creed, but I'd almost forgotten how stubborn he could be, and he didn't need to get into hot water with the local authorities the first day he arrived in town.

"You don't seriously believe what he's saying," Creed whispered to me as I dragged him to the other side of the mine.

"Of course not. But there's no point in arguing about it."

"Although..." Magnus leaned closer to make sure his words were only for us. Even Trent and Ellis, who were inspecting another part of the mine a few steps away, wouldn't be able to hear him. "It is strange. How were the Milford sisters able to find such a mineable area that no one else knew about?"

Creed crossed his arms, staring down at the floor with a harsh glare. "Maybe they could read the land and knew there were resources in this area, and that's why they came to this town. Or maybe they just got lucky. Whatever the real answer, we're never gonna know, but it certainly wasn't magic."

"Speaking of unknown answers," I nudged Creed's shoulder. "You still haven't told us how you ended up here in the first place. Last we'd heard, you'd been captured, but possibly rescued. We haven't been able to get a straight answer out of anyone concerning you, so you'd better give us an explanation."

Creed looked away before he answered, a clear sign that I wasn't going to like what he said.

"I ended up getting captured because of the incompetence of my superiors, but luckily, I was rescued after only a short time. The military then let me retire early as compensation, although it's really just a bribe so that I won't sue them for their negligence. That was fine with me, plus I have POW status now, so I accepted the deal."

Magnus and I stared at each other for a moment. Based on the look in his eye, I could tell we were thinking the same thing.

"Creed," I said hesitantly. "Did you arrange your own capture so that you could manipulate the military into letting you retire a few months early."

The expression on Creed's face never changed as he returned our pointed stares. But something indecipherable shifted behind his eyes. "Legally, I'm required to say no."

Which meant *yes*. It was as I suspected. Creed really had orchestrated his own disappearance. I would have been furious with him for worrying us like that, but I was also grateful for the outcome.

Clearing his throat, Creed pulled out something from his pocket and held it up to the light. "Anyway. More importantly, what is this?" He held out the wooden dowel that had been hidden inside Poppy Milford's vault.

Grabbing the dowel, I turned it over in my hands. "I forgot about this. It was stored inside Poppy Milford's vault. Ellis and I were both almost killed for this damn piece of wood."

Even up close, it still didn't look like anything important. A part of me wanted to chuck it down into the deepest depths of the mine, where it could remain lost forever, but I resisted. Even if it didn't look important, it must have been stashed in that vault for a reason.

As simply as we could, Magnus and I explained everything to Creed. He was just as confused as we were about the situation, and none of us had any idea why the sisters had gone to such great lengths to hide such a random object.

We still hadn't come up with any answers when Deputy Hillard came up to us, saying that the rest of the tunnels had been searched and so far, there didn't seem to be any other cult members lurking around.

I quickly stashed the dowel in my pocket before Deputy Hillard or any of the officers could see it. Just because I didn't know its importance yet, I also wasn't going to relinquish it to anyone else. Ellis and I had almost died for it, so as far as I was concerned, we were the most deserving to keep it.

So many questions still remained, but it was clear we weren't going to get any more answers. We were free to go home, safe in the knowledge that our attackers had been stopped and the danger had passed.

For now.

CHAPTER FOURTEEN

Ellis

AFTER FINALLY GETTING back to Brody's house, the two of us immediately fell into bed. The short nap we'd taken in the middle of the tunnel was the only sleep we'd had for nearly a day and a half, so we were exhausted. We didn't even have the energy to wash off the dirt from the tunnels.

So, when we finally woke up and felt like functioning people again, our first order of business was a bath.

Together, of course. When building his house, Brody had installed a particularly large tub in his bathroom that was big enough for both of us, and I was eager to take advantage of it.

I couldn't remember the last time I'd taken a bath with another person. Maybe when I was a young child, when my mother bathed my brother and me at the same time.

It was a bittersweet memory, but I was finally able to think about my brother without immediately wanting to break out crying—or punch something—so I figured that meant I was making progress.

Plus, bathing with Brody was much more enjoyable.

The bathtub was completely circular, so there was no right way or wrong way to sit in it. We were positioned facing each other, legs tangled together as we lounged among the hot water and bubbles floating on the surface. Steam welled up around us to the point that the rest of the bathroom was barely visible.

"So, I'm still not entirely sure what happened," I said as I idly stirred my fingers across the surface of the water. "So, the Milford sisters were born into *The Tamed Souls* cult. Escaped that cult. Stole something from the cult leader on their way out. Came to Emberwood, where they were adopted by the Milford family, and a new cult was formed around them when they predicted a fire, found resources to mine, and other 'miraculous' things. Then the previous cult leader comes looking for whatever they stole, ends up dead, and his body turns up buried in the foundation of your property. Do I have that right?"

Brody nodded while keeping his head leaning back against the edge of the tub. "That's about right."

His red hair was wet and looked darker than normal, making it contrast more starkly against his pale skin. I was distracted for a moment, watching water droplets slowly slide down his neck and chest.

My arousal twitched in the hot water, and I shook myself back to my senses.

"But we still don't know what the sisters stole, why they tried so hard to hide it, and why the cult leader—what was his name? Angus Grieve—wanted it back so bad. Nor do we understand the meaning behind the coffee beans in Rose's locket, or the wooden dowel in Poppy's vault."

Once again, Brody confirmed that I'd gotten everything right.

Somehow, despite having all the right information, I still felt like I didn't know anything. It was like finally putting together all the edges pieces of a puzzle, but still having no idea what the final product was supposed to be. Even if I didn't have all the pieces in place, I should at least be able to tell what image I was trying to create.

Brody rubbed his leg against mine under the water, distracting me from my thoughts. "Don't worry about it so much. We'll figure things out. For now, just take time to relax."

That sounded like a good idea, but then, as Brody's leg brushed against me again, an even better thought came to me.

I climbed across the tub, moving slowly to avoid disturbing the water too much, until I straddled his lap. "Or we could do the opposite of relaxing."

Apparently, it was an easy decision because Brody didn't think very long before he grabbed me. Water splashed over the edge of the tub as he pulled me into a kiss. My knees slid against the bottom of the tub under water, and I braced my hands against his chest for support to keep from falling right on top of him.

Pretending to support me, Brody grabbed my ass hard enough to bruise. He then slid one hand down to my thighs to squeeze the generous flesh there, while he pressed his other hand between my ass cheeks to slip one finger inside me. Warm water followed his finger, making me gasp from the strange feeling, as if my muscles were liquefying.

Brody swallowed every sound I made, continuing to move his fingers inside me until I was writhing with his touch and kneading against his chest like an overgrown cat.

"I was thinking," he said when he finally pulled away from the kiss. "If you want me to go get protection, I can. Though, I'll have to get out of the tub. However, if you're comfortable, we could go without it."

I was still panting after the intense kiss, sucking in deep gulps of steamy air. It took me a moment to realize what he was saying, but Brody was content to simply sit there and continue toying with me as he waited for my brain to start working again.

Eventually, I managed to nod.

"Does that mean you want me to go fetch some stuff, or that you trust me to go without it?"

"I... I trust you."

I'd already trusted this man with my life numerous times. Trusting him with my health was no concern after that.

All of a sudden, Brody pulled his fingers from my body, and I was left empty and wanting. My cock was already dripping pre-come into the bath water, desperate for attention.

"Turn around," Brody said, with one more firm squeeze to my ass.

The tub was circular, so there was no 'front' or 'back' to face. I wasn't sure what direction he wanted me to turn, but luckily, he was willing to guide me. Large, gentle hands repositioned me until I was bent over the edge of the tub. My legs were still in the water, and my hands were braced on the tiled bathroom floor, which left my ass on full display in the air.

The whole bathroom was filled with steam, but the air was still colder than the heated water. I shivered as goosebumps erupted all over my body, but I didn't move from where I'd been placed.

Brody nipped at my shoulder with his teeth. It wasn't hard enough to break skin, not even enough to leave a mark, and was more like a reminder of pain than an actual sensation.

"If I can't leave the tub, then that means we don't have any lube, either," he said directly into my ear, before placing a kiss over the spot that he just nipped. "I hope you can handle a rough ride."

I might have nodded or made some

sort of sound in agreement. I couldn't tell. My brain already felt like it had been invaded by the steam filling the room and turned all my thoughts to mush. His fingers found their way back inside me, carefully opening me up. The bathwater provided some lubricant, but not much, and the burn of the extra friction made my hips jerk as I tried to pull away and press closer at the same time. My cock rubbed against the smooth edge of the tub, and I sunk my teeth into my own forearm to silence my moans, which were echoing off the walls of the bathroom.

A hand tangled into my hair and pulled my head back, freeing my mouth from my arm.

"Oh, no. Don't silence yourself. I want to hear every sound you make."

Without proper lube, it was slow going. Brody took his time, carefully stretching me open until he was certain I was ready for him. Meanwhile, my voice bounced off the wall as I begged him to hurry up.

I would have been embarrassed by my own voice if I was able to feel anything other than desperation and burning arousal.

When he finally pressed inside of me, he moved slowly. Inch by inch, his cock carved a path through me, drawing out the sensation until the pleasure was on the edge of turning into pain. I tried pushing back against him, eager for him to hurry and fill me, but my hands slid over the white tiles of the floor.

It was almost worse than being bound. My limbs were completely free to move but couldn't do anything useful. Most of my weight rested on my stomach, and the edge of the tub bit into my hips as Brody finally slid into me all the way. He gripped onto the edge of the tub for stability, his hands pinning me even more in place, before pulling out and slamming back inside all at once.

BRODY

He set a punishing pace. More water sloshed over the side of the tub onto the floor with each thrust of his hips. Wet flesh smacked against wet flesh, filling the bathroom with the echoes of our coupling.

I dug my fingers into the groves of the floor tile, desperate for some form of traction to help me withstand the force as he thrust inside me. My insides felt scraped raw, and oversensitive nerves sent pleasure tingling up my spine every time Brody moved.

It was too perfect for words. The ecstasy that burned through my veins felt like a cleansing fire, eradicating every doubt, every negative thought that had ever existed before this moment.

This was where I belonged.

With a sudden, piercing jolt of electric pleasure, I came with a shout. My climax spilled over the edge of the tub and onto the bathroom tile, white staining white.

A moment later, Brody followed as

well. Without the extra layer of protection that had always separated us before, I felt his heat more than usual. It flooded me, filling me up right down to my core so not an inch of me remained that wasn't claimed by him.

Something in my brain stopped working. I didn't pass out, but I completely froze. Even my thoughts went dark. Brody eventually had to guide me back into the tub, settling me against his chest as he let the warm water soothe my abused muscles.

The steam around us slowly disappeared, allowing me to see parts of the bathroom walls again. It was like waking up from a dream. One by one, the synapses in my brain reconnected until I was eventually able to complete a thought.

Looking up at Brody, who had never once let me go, I smiled.

"Again?"

***

It was hours before we finished. After the water in the bath grew cold, we moved to the bedroom and continued there. By the time we collapsed onto the mattress, spent and exhausted, it was late into the night. We didn't say anything as we lay shoulder to shoulder and Brody intertwined his fingers with mine. In that moment, it felt like we were the only two people in the world, and I was content to stay in that very spot forever.

The moment was broken by the sound of a fist banging on the bedroom door.

"Are you two done, yet?" Creed's voice shouted through the door. "I can hear you from the guest room, and some of us want to sleep tonight."

I froze, mortification pouring through me as I realized that Creed had heard everything we'd done. I'd gotten so used to the idea of Brody's house being our own sanctuary that I'd completely forgotten that Creed was now staying in the guest bedroom, which wasn't far away.

Beside me, Brody groaned and threw an arm over his eyes like he was trying to block out the rest of the world. "This is my house," he shouted back at Creed. "You're just a guest here. We can do whatever we want, for as long as we want. If you've got a problem with it, then Magnus has a guest bedroom as well."

Even through the door I could hear the sound of Creed's scoff. "Magnus? Please. He's even louder than you."

Grabbing one of the pillows off the bed, Brody threw it at the door where it made a surprisingly loud thump against the wood. "Then count your blessings and keep your complaints to yourself."

"All right, all right," Creed grumbled. "And here I thought you were the more sensible one."

"You're just jealous you're the only one

not getting laid."

The comment was harsh, but there was an undertone of affection in it.

On the other side of the door, Creed started laughing.

"Whatever you need to tell yourself to sleep at night. Although, it seems like you won't be doing much of that."

Brody threw another pillow at the door, which just made Creed laugh harder before we heard his footsteps as he walked away.

Flopping back onto the bed, Brody buried his face into the last remaining pillow.

"Fuuuuuck."

I tentatively placed a hand on his shoulder. "I'm sure it's not that bad. I mean, he was laughing, so I don't think he was upset."

Not lifting his face from the pillow, Brody shook his head. "No. It's not that. This is hardly the first time one of us has overheard the other. Hell, there has been a few times where we've walked in on each other with a partner. At least this time the door was locked."

"Then what's the problem?"

Finally, Brody lifted his face from the pillow, and I could see that his blue-green eyes were sparkling with his own laughter.

"I'm going to have to start building Creed's house right away. He's not staying here any longer than necessary."

Then Brody started laughing for real.

I joined him in his laughter, promising to help however I could with the construction. We continued to lie there for a while longer, keeping our voices down to a whisper as we made more plans for the future. The best part of the whole night was the assumption that I'd be moving in with Brody. There wasn't even a discussion. I was already so established in Brody's home that living anywhere else was unthinkable.

It felt good, finally having a home. I couldn't remember the last time I was so accepted somewhere. Even before my brother got sick, it always felt like I was just floating from place to place, waiting for the next gust of wind to send me on my way like a dandelion seed drifting through the air.

Now, finally, I'd landed somewhere comfortable, and for the first time in my life, I could start putting down my own roots.

Click now to read *Creed*, the next book in the Rock Hard Mountain Men series.

Dear Reader,

THANK YOU for reading Brody, book two in the Rock Hard Mountain Men series.

If you enjoyed this taste of brawny, hairy alpha men who once lived to serve their country, and now strive for nothing more than a simple life with some peace and quiet—yet seem to attract action and mystery, and perhaps a little bit of man on man lovin' along the way, then please let me know.

You can simply return to the online retailer where you made your purchase and leave me a short review.

Your thoughts may just encourage other readers to try my books, and help me continue writing the characters we all adore and root for.

Even a few words would mean the world to me.

☺

~Love, Evie Riley

OTHER BOOKS BY EVIE

My action-filled, romantic suspense, and darker-themed books:

Rock Hard Mountain Men
Magnus
Brody
Creed

Ruthless Empire
Courting Danger
Chasing Danger
Kissing Danger

Federal Protection Agency
Mason
Rafe
Ryzen
Cooper
Noah
Damien
Sebastian

EVIE RILEY

Gabe
Logan

Smokejumpers
Hawke
Cyrus
Jase
Gage
Jackson
Xavier

From The Edge
Shattered
Runaway
Jaded
Rescue
Hidden
Tormented

Gray Vale Pack
His Fated Mate
His Wounded Warrior
His Healing Heart

My more romance-themed books:

Rock His World

Hollow Heart

Wild Stars

Grave Misgivings

Jasper Springs

Cade

Dawson

Drew

Grayson

Riley

Mitch

ABOUT THE AUTHOR

Evie Riley believes too much time spent at the beach is barely enough. She enjoys spending time puttering in the garden, cooking yummy things for her family, and has a quirky personality, described by her partner as ranging from cute to deadly, depending on her blood-chocolate levels.

Evie crafts steamy gay male romance filled with all the edgy angst, or dark and gritty romantic suspense where her men must overcome difficult obstacles and may find love along the way while dishing out their own brand of justice.

Evie spends her nights writing bad boys in love, and her days wrangling the sweet boys she loves.

EVIE RILEY
ER
PUTTING THE MM IN YUMMY